Wilson Katiyo was [...] Zimbabwe. From an early age he went to live and work with many different members of his family. In 1965, he was arrested for one month. After being released he was helped by friends to escape from Rhodesia to Zambia. Befriended by the Hodgkin family in Lusaka, he was able to travel to Britain and continue his studies. *A Son of the Soil* is a semi-autobiographical account of his life and escape.

Wilson Katiyo has now returned to Zimbabwe and continues to write. His second novel *Going to Heaven*, also published by LONGMAN, is a sequel to *A Son of the Soil*.

A Son
of the
Soil

Wilson Katiyo

Longman

For Elizabeth Hodgkin

Longman Group UK Limited
Longman House, Burnt Mill
Harlow, Essex CM20 2JE, England
and Associated Companies throughout the world.

© Wilson Katiyo 1976

First published in Longman African Classic 1988
Third impression 1989

Produced by Longman Group (FE) Ltd.
Printed in Hong Kong

ISBN 0 582 02656 3

BOOK ONE: IN THE BEGINNING . . .

OUR VILLAGE—CHIEF MAKOSA'S village, was on a broad water-shed between two valleys; one lay to the east and the other to the south-west of the village. The village itself, like most other villages, was made up of clusters of several hundred small round mud-and-thatch huts, which were scattered all over the plateau. The majority of the people, again like any other villagers in the land, were subsistence farmers by trade. Their lives revolved around their fields which spread out on the eastern side of the village, across the valley. Also closely involved with their everyday way of life was the dense bush which almost enclosed the village in all directions but the east. Somehow, everything: the village, the valleys, the thick bush and the fertile brown fields were all in turn surrounded by hills and mountains. There was the hazy mountain range, which looked almost blue, in the distant north; closer to the village in the east, stood the conical red-earth hills; to the south and to the west were situated the non-uniform granite hills. For most of the villagers, it was these hills and that mountain range which marked the boundary of the world.

For some time now, everyone in the village had known that a man named Sekuru was quite ill. People had also known that there was not much anybody could do for him. Sekuru was now very much in his old age. Therefore, perhaps, people could not have been expected to be overly concerned about the health of an old man. But they were. Every morning before most people left for the fields, and every evening after their return, there was a constant stream of the young and the old, men and women, all going in and coming out of the old man's hut. Nobody, except some members of his immediate family and a few close friends of his generation, stayed inside the hut for very long. One after another, each visitor (and at times two or three), pushed open the twig-knitted door and entered the hut. Inside the dark hut, the visitor found the black-and-white haired old man either sitting down on a rush-mat spread in front of a small fire or lying on the mat with his small brown eyes peering towards the entrance to the hut. After sitting on the floor, the visitor greeted the old man whom, to show respect for his age in a traditional manner, everyone addressed as grandfather.

'How do you feel today, Grandfather?'

'Who is this?' asked Sekuru in his now weak husky voice.

'It's me—Tigere.'

'Who?'

'Tigere!—Katsande's son!'

The old man spoke slowly and very deliberately:

'Ah! My friend. Forgive me. My eyes are not good anymore . . . I did not recognize you . . . How was your day?'

'Much the same as usual! Much the same as usual at this time of the year, Grandfather.'

'What did you say?—Come closer so I can hear you . . .'

The visitor moved closer to Sekuru,

'I said at this time of the year, one day is the same as another! There is too much work at the fields!'

'True, indeed. There is too much work at the fields at this time of the year . . . But you are a hard worker, Tigere. A good worker!'

'. . . And you, Grandfather. How do you feel today?'

'Ooo. As you can just see. The same. More or less. The same . . . And your family, are they all well?'

'Quite well, Grandfather! Quite well indeed! Except for too much work, of course!'

'Indeed. How is my friend Katsande?'

'I thought father said he was passing through this way to see you this morning on his way to the fields?'

'This morning? . . . Oh! Yes, of course. He did stop by this morning, I remember now.'

'Grandfather, is there anything you would like me to fetch you now or to bring you next time I come?'

'No, my friend. No. I have everything I need—my firewood and my snuff. That's all I need these days! They all bring me plenty of firewood and the best snuff. I have every blend of snuff. Shall we—shall we take some?'

'I don't take any, Grandfather!'

'Oh? . . . I keep forgetting . . . But I will tell you something: you will when you get older . . . They tell me Goredema passed away?'

'Yes, Grandfather! It was very sad!'

'Indeed . . . Indeed.—Would you pass me another log to put on the fire? . . . Thank you. Yes. About Goredema—The way the spirits of the ancestors work! Gore was just a boy—I mean he was so much younger than some of us. But there he goes before even me! . . . I don't know what happens to the blood when one gets old. You know, it's the blood that keeps your body warm. But when you get to be as old as some of us, a fire becomes a god. Even the noon-day heat. It doesn't keep me warm enough anymore . . .'

'Well, Grandfather, I must go and light a fire at my "*dare*"! I hope you will sleep well. I may see you tomorrow or the day after tomorrow.'

'Thank you for coming to see me, Tigere. I know I am not much company anymore, but come again. It's kind of you . . . And don't forget to greet my friend, your grandfather, for me.'

'No, Grandfather, I shall not!'

The visitor came out of the hut closing the door behind him. And the next visitor opened the twig-matted door.

Sekuru was one of the most reputable medicine-men not only at Makosa's village but also throughout the area. The art of medicine had been passed on to him by his grandfather. Sekuru had been the favourite grandchild of his grandfather and when still a boy, Sekuru had spent much time with the old man. Together, they used to get up before sunrise and go to comb the bush for herbs. Sekuru had observed carefully as his grandfather prepared and administered the herbs. By the time his grandfather died, Sekuru was already a good medicine-man in his own right. As time passed, Sekuru's reputation not only surpassed that of his grandfather and other contemporary medicine-men but also that of his grandfather's father who had been an eminent medicine-man as well. In fact, Sekuru became so well-known that many people, some coming from as far as four or even five day's walk away, had, until recently, regularly arrived at Makosa's village in order to seek his help. Of course, all this reputation reflected very well indeed the success Sekuru had had in helping other people.

Besides being a most reputable medicine-man, the old man

had also been the medium through whom the spirits of the ancestors and the spirits of the deceased had communicated with the living. Not all medicine-men were necessarily mediums, nor were the few mediums in the land necessarily medicine-men. It was this exceptional position of being both a medicine-man and a medium that made Sekuru such a revered person at Makosa's village. Whenever rains failed, as they did once in every seven or so years, it was to Sekuru that Chief Makosa, other sub-chiefs and the people of the region had turned. On such occasions people would gather outside Sekuru's huts to sing and dance to drums. Elders would chant the liturgy and implore the spirits of the ancestors to give them rain. This would go on until Sekuru was possessed by the spirit of the lion. The spirits of the ancestors resided in the body of a lion when not communicating with the living. They controlled the character and nature of that lion. So, when the people invoked the spirits of the ancestors and Sekuru became possessed, he behaved and acted just like a lion—a lion with a wounded paw. More often than not, these gatherings outside Sekuru's hut ended with people dispersing under very heavy showers. At other times, however, the people had to go away and give some offering to the spirits of the ancestors before any rain would fall. As a medium, Sekuru had many other duties.

Sekuru had also had a number of other responsibilities in the village. Some of these had to do with his being a medium or a medicine-man but others didn't. He had led the village in some of the traditional ceremonies—such as the offering ceremonies and the consecrations of the spirits of the recently deceased. He had been a village elder and Chief Makosa's close confidant and counsellor. Together with other village elders, Chief Makosa and Sekuru had tried many offenders and settled hundreds of land, marriage and a variety of other disputes that had taken place in the village.

A number of marriages in the village owed their existance to Sekuru. Both young and middle-aged men taking their first, or second or third or even fourth wives had begged Sekuru to be their middle-man. Sekuru had not always been willing to be a middle-man; especially in those marriages where, in his well-respected judgement, there had been no prospect of harmony.

Sekuru himself could have taken as many wives as he pleased, but he had contented himself with only three. With his first wife, Ma Gomo, he had had a son, a daughter, a son, a second daughter, two sons, another daughter and three more sons. Ma Tsindi, the second wife had given him a son, two daughters, another son, a daughter and two more sons. Sekuru had had only one child, a son, with his youngest and third wife, Ma Rugare. Unfortunately, she had died before they could have more children. However, the rest of the family had lived harmoniously together in one big yard. Sekuru's own hut and his *dare* were situated in the middle of the yard and were surrounded by his wives' and children's huts.

Now, Sekuru never went out of his hut except two or three times a day when nature called. Only then, stooping heavily and gripping, as firmly as an infant might grip its mother's finger, the walking-stick upon which the weight of the left-overs of his once tall and elegant body rested, would he be seen tottering between his hut and an acacia shrub at the edge of the yard. Every few steps, he would pause to rest. By the time he walked back into his soot-matted hut, the old man would be very tired. Almost everything seemed to tire him now. Even talking. Gone, forever, was the time when the best part of the day for him was the evening. For it was then, after taking the evening meal and surrounded by the younger of his children, his older grandchildren and their many friends that Sekuru used to settle down at his *dare* and enjoy his favourite pastime: story telling.

'The story I am going to tell you tonight, I know, will not amuse or entertain you much,' he would begin a story after the struggle to sit as close to him as possible by the eager children had ceased.

'But then, not everything in life is amusing or entertaining. I want you all to sit quietly and listen very carefully . . .'

Once upon a time, there was a certain village. The chief of this village was named Chuma. Chuma's village was a very ordinary village. One day, it was towards the evening as most people in Chuma's village were arriving from their fields, some very strange visitors arrived in the village. There were many of these strange visitors—maybe as many as one hundred. The visitors gathered at Chief Chuma's huts. What was strange about the visitors was that they were white men. Of course white men could not be strange to you because you have all seen quite a few. But for Chief Chuma and his people, this was the first time anyone of them had set eyes on any white man. This was because no white man had ever set foot in their village before.

At first, as you can imagine, the people were a little frightened but also a little fascinated by the appearance of the white men. As more people arrived from the fields, they gathered and watched the white men from a distance. People wondered who these 'men' were—if they were men at all. Where had they come from? Where were they going? Why had they come to Chuma's village? You know what happens with a curious crowd: people began edging closer and closer to Chief Chuma's huts in order to have a better look at the white men. But before they got too near, a young man named Shonga had a thought.

'Assuming these white men are invaders, they wouldn't let Chief Chuma sound the war drum, would they? I am not saying they are. But we don't know. The best thing would be to find out,' he said.

Everybody agreed with him. But how could they find out? An elder provided the solution. He asked for a volunteer and Shonga immediately offered himself before anyone else. The volunteer was to walk over to Chief Chuma's huts, stay there for a certain length of time and then come back to inform the people what was going on.

But before the volunteer went over, the elder suggested that all warriors should go to their huts and fetch their spears, axes, bows and arrows. To avoid alerting and therefore provoking the white men, only a few warriors at a time were to leave and come back before the next lot left. The elder warned all warriors to conceal their weapons as much as possible. In order to hide the movement of the warriors and to help conceal the weapons, women and children were told to move to the fore of the crowd. A few warriors lived on the other side of Chief Chuma's huts. Therefore it was impossible for them to get to their huts and bring their weapons without being seen by the white men. It could be done, but it would take much time. Some of them borrowed weapons but others simply stood with the women and children. When most of the warriors had returned with their weapons, Shonga walked off to Chief Chuma's huts.

Shonga avoided passing too close to the white men. As he approached Chief Chuma's home, he observed that the white men had many horses and six ox-drawn waggons. Among the white men, he noticed seven young black men. He guessed that the black men did the job of driving the ox-waggons. When he arrived at the huts, Chief Chuma was seated at his dare. A black man was translating for Chief Chuma and a white man. As Shonga learned later, the white man was called Hill. He was the leader of the white men.

'There is nothing wrong with our twenty-four oxen except that they are very tired. We need fresh oxen. You lose nothing,' the white man was saying to Chief Chuma.

'As I have already said, I myself don't have twenty-four oxen, otherwise we would exchange. I can't just order any man to exchange his oxen for yours. I have to talk to the village elders to see how we can all help. And why do you want seventeen of our young men?'

'We want them to work for us. We will pay them well.'

'Again, that's not up to me. It's up to the parents of the young men and the men themselves.'

'All right. For the last time, I am offering to exchange twenty-four oxen. For only seventeen men, I shall give you two guns and a lot of bullets, two shirts, a pair of trousers, and on top of all that, a mirror! . . . What do you say?'

'I said I need to consult my people!' Shouted the Chief.

'Don't you shout at me! What you don't seem to realize is that I can simply take as many oxen and as many men as I want!'

It was at this point that Shonga felt he had stayed long enough and he had heard enough. So he started walking back to where the people were. But the white man, 'Boss' Hill, as he liked to be called, pointed a small gun at him and ordered him to stop. The crowd which was still edging closer to the Chief's huts, clearly saw what was happening. The women and the children got out of the way of the warriors and ran—away from the Chief's huts. When the white men heard this commotion, they prepared their guns. As the warriors surged forward, the white men began firing. Several warriors fell. Chief Chuma rushed forward and pleaded with 'Boss' Hill to order his men to stop the shooting. The Chief offered to order his warriors to cease the attack in return. The white man agreed. Hill ordered his men to stop firing and Chief Chuma commanded his warriors to cease the attack. After this, Hill ordered all his men to mount their horses. Most people thought the white men were about to leave. But instead, the man, 'Boss' Hill pointed his gun at Chief Chuma and told him to order his warriors to heap their weapons on the ground. Fearing for his life, Chief Chuma obeyed. All the warriors lay down their weapons. Then, Hill motioned his men to surround the warriors. The white men had their guns pointed at the warriors.

Next, Hill ordered two of his men, one white and the other black, to force Shonga to lead them to the cattle pens. They were to find and bring twenty-four fit oxen. Meanwhile, Hill himself walked among the surrounded and disarmed warriors picking out strong young men. He selected twenty warriors and separated them from the rest. As soon as Shonga and the two men returned with a herd of twenty-four oxen, the fresh set of oxen was yoked. Hill shot dead all the twenty-four oxen that had been unyoked. After that the white men with their booty of twenty-four oxen, twenty-one young men, (including Shonga) and four of the killed oxen, marched out of the village towards the north.

After the departure of the white men, the village gathered and began mourning the dead. In all, there were forty warriors dead; and eleven had been wounded. After three days of mourning, the dead were buried. The grieving Chief and elders gathered to discuss what to do next. Nobody knew where the white men had come from or where they had gone to. *It was debated whether to pursue them or not. Of course there were a number of difficulties. It was all very well following the white men in the northerly direction but that did not mean they might not have changed directions. The white men had horses and ox-waggons. In three days they would be a long way from Chuma's village. Even if the warriors caught up with the white men, the white men could always threaten to kill all the young men who had been taken. Of course, nobody wanted that to happen. Therefore, it was decided not to pursue the white men. The only hope was that the captured men, since they were all young and strong, would escape from the white men when a chance presented itself. So it was left to the young men to liberate themselves.*

Many days passed without any news of the men. Relatives kept watchful eyes at the path on the northern side of the village. But it remained quiet and bare. Weeks, months and eventually a year of much anguish passed and still there was no news about the young men. By now, everyone had forgotten about the oxen. Some families began discussing having funeral ceremonies for their sons as there was no hope of ever seeing them again.

Then one day, a small boy who was herding his family's cattle sighted a white man on the outskirts of Chuma's village. He ran to his father, who was at home tanning leather for drums, and informed about the white man. The father hurried to Chief Chuma's dare and reported the presence of the white man. It was at the beginning of the autumn and most people had finished harvesting. So most warriors were about the village. Chief Chuma did not want to alert the white man by sounding the war drum. Instead, he sent out three of his sons to call up as many warriors as they could in the shortest possible time. Indeed, in a very short time, there were forty warriors at Chief Chuma's dare. He ordered four of them to go and capture the white man and to bring him to the Chief's dare. The four warriors ran towards where the white man had been seen. But they did not have to go out of the village because the white man was already approaching the village. They captured him and his bundle of belongings and brought him before Chief Chuma. In the meantime, some of the

warriors had been sent to call village elders as well as more
warriors. Chief Chuma did not know whether the white man
had come to the village alone or with other whites. As a
precaution, he deployed his warriors around the village. The
white man, who was now standing before the Chief and the
elders, was shaking like a river reed with fear.

'What do you want in our village?' Chief Chuma
demanded. To the surprise of everyone, the white man began
to answer in our language.

'My name is Rev Mills. I come from England. I am here on
God's work and I come in peace and with goodwill—'

'The question I asked you is: what do you want here in our
village?'

'I think if I am allowed to explain, it will be easier—'

'Where are you arriving from?'

'From Mtoko's village.'

'And where are you going?'

'I come here to your village.'

'Why have you come here?'

'I have come to seek for your permission to open a mission
here in your village.'

'What is a mission?'

'Ah! That's what I meant by saying it would be easier to
understand if I am allowed to explain first—'

'On your journey from Mtoko's village, did you travel
alone?'

'Yes, Sire.'

'And you did not see any other white men on your way?'

'No. None at all.'

'Are there any white men at Mtoko's village?'

'There are quite a number. They are all mineral
hunters—They dig a diamond mine there.'

'. . . Elders, you all hear what this white is saying.'

'Indeed!! Indeed!!' they all replied.

'Now, tell us. You say you came here by yourself?'

'That is as it is, Chief Chuma.'

'How did you know your way here?'

'I was given very good directions before I started—'

'By white men who have been in my village before?'

'No, Chief Chuma. By my assistant. You should know him. His name is Shonga. He comes from—'

'Shonga?! Did you say Shonga?!'

'Yes. We work together. We are very good friends. In fact, it was Shonga—'

'Shonga is alive?'

'I beg to be allowed to explain. You see—'

'You have a lot to explain! Begin from when you first met Shonga. Tell us everything!'

'Well, there is not much to tell,' Mills began.

The white man had arrived at Mtoko's village the year before. On his arrival there, he had met some white mineral hunters. They, especially their leader, a man named Hill, had been very kind to Mills, so he said. He had stayed some weeks with the mineral hunters before he decided to open a mission at Mtoko's village. Mills needed a black man who would translate for him. The good friend, Hill, had 'given' him the black man he needed. This black man was of course Shonga.

At first Shonga couldn't understand or speak English well. But in time, Mills and Shonga taught each other the others' language. In time, Shonga was converted to Christianity. It was also Shonga who had built the three huts the two men now shared at Mtoko's village. Also the small church which now stood in the village. Things were going very well at Mtoko. Soon there was to be a mission school and a clinic. It was Shonga who had suggested that Rev Mills come to Chuma's village and see whether it was possible to open a mission.

'That is how I came to know Shonga.'

'Did Shonga ever tell you how he left his village?'

'Yes, but not in great detail. I think he said that they had been more or less forcibly recruited to work in the mines. But I must assure you that Shonga and the rest of the men from this village are very happy. The other men are working in the mines. My friend Hill treats them very well. He pays them for their work.'

'Elders, we shall talk about the children of our village in a short while. But first, we must finish with this white man . . . Tell us Rev Mills, what is a mission?'

'Sire, I left my home in England to come to this great land in order to help other people. As a Christian, I believe in God through his only Son, the Lord Jesus Christ. If we opened a mission here, everyone in this village would have a chance to learn His teachings, which unless followed, means that there is no other way into the Almighty's Kingdom. So, I am asking for your permission to build a church here in your village so that you and your people may have the opportunity to worship God. Indeed, when the Day of Judgement comes, I don't want to see even one person in this village go to burn in the eternal fire of Hell. I hope and pray that you will all see the light so that when the Day of Judgement comes, you will all sit with our Lord Jesus Christ and enjoy the life without end, in Heaven.'

'In time, we would also like to open a mission school and a clinic. Your children would be taught to read and to write. They would be taught about other people and other lands. We would teach them to love others, to give to others and to be kind to others. I see there is much disease among your people. We would open the clinic as soon as—'

'What we have heard is enough. I do not understand what you are saying. But the way we live here is like this. When anyone dies, their spirit joins the spirits of the ancestors. There is no doubt that besides having much power over us all, the spirits of the ancestors and the deceased have a good everlasting life . . . It seems to me you want us to worship your King.—Is his name God?'

'Well—'

'What is the purpose of our children learning to read and write? They don't need your school to know to love or to give or to be kind. Besides, who do you think will look after the cattle and goats while our children go to your school? In this village, we have several eminent medicine-men. We do not need your medicine.'

Mills was taken in one of Chief Chuma's huts while the Chief and the elders discussed what to do with him. Mills had confessed a friendship with Hill who had killed warriors and taken away twenty-one young men of the village. Some of the elders felt that Mills should be killed. But others couldn't accept this decision because they thought it was not just. After much debate, Chief Chuma decided that the best thing to do was to consult the eminent village medicine-men. The medicine-men were then summoned to Chief Chuma's dare.

One after another, each medicine-man was brought before Chief Chuma and the elders. Each tossed his hakatas after being asked what was to be done with Mills. And without exception, the medicine-men foretold a great misfortune for the whole village if Mills was killed. They recommended that he be banished from the village. Chief Chuma and all the elders accepted this decision. Mills was brought back to Chief Chuma's dare where he was simply told to leave and never to set foot in Chuma's village again. Warriors escorted him on to the path that led to Mtoko's village.

As people heard later, Mills had walked to Mtoko throughout that night. When he finally arrived at Mtoko, he was very tired. So he went into his hut and fell into a deep sleep. Nobody at Mtoko, not even Shonga, knew of Mills' return from Chuma's village.

At about midday the following day, still unaware that Mills had returned, Shonga was sitting in their church reading a Bible. Suddenly, a little boy, panting and looking frightened ran up to Shonga and informed him that a group of white men were approaching the village. Many groups of white men had visited Rev Mills at Mtoko's village before. But this was the first time Shonga had ever been left in charge of the mission at Mtoko. He had never dealt with any of the visiting groups of white men in the absence of Rev Mills. So Shonga became frightened. How was he going to manage the situation? He decided that the best thing to do was to ask the villagers to gather. So he ran around the village asking people to assemble at the church. Soon enough, most of the villagers were gathered outside the church.

He addressed the villagers:

'There are white men coming here. As you all know, many groups of white men have visited us before. You have yourselves seen that they are good men. They mean us no harm. Indeed in the eyes of the Lord, they are our brothers. I know that most of you don't believe in God. But let us *welcome these white men as our brothers. When they arrive, I beg you all to say to them, "Welcome brothers!" three times.'*

As the group of white men, riding on horses, came close to the church, Shonga immediately recognized the white man Hill. When Hill and his men came to a halt, Shonga realized that they were very drunk. Hill and his men never went anywhere without their guns.

'Welcome brothers! Welcome brothers! Welcome brothers!' roared the crowd of villagers without any warmth in their voices. Shonga stepped forward, knelt down and greeted Hill in the usual traditional way.

'Stand up, boy!' ordered Hill.

Shonga obeyed.

'Did your Boss, Mills, leave yesterday?'

'Yes, Boss,' replied Shonga humbly.

'Did he say when he was coming back?'

'No Boss.'

'Good!' said Hill as he pulled out a bottle of whisky from a bag tied around his waist. He drank some whisky out of it before passing it on to his men.

'All right, boys. The town is ours!' Hill said to his men as he got off his horse.

'Hurray!!' 'Hurray!!' the white men shouted and got off their horses as well.

'Hey, boy,' Hill called Shonga.

'Yes, Boss?'

'Can you count?'

'Yes, Boss.'

'Then I want you to count how many white men you see.'

'Twenty-two, Boss,' announced Shonga after a while.

'How many?'

'Twenty-two.'

'Now, don't you get cheeky with me, boy!'

Shonga didn't understand what he had done wrong.

'How many?'

'Twenty-two white men.'

'You used to be a very good boy, Shonga. But now I can see that Mills has spoiled you. You are losing your good manners. Come here!'

Shonga walked the few feet to where Hill was standing. Hill glared at Shonga for some seconds before hitting him across the face with the back of his hand. Shonga fell backwards. The white men laughed.

'The correct way to answer is: "Twenty-two, Boss." Understand?!'

'Yes, Boss,' replied a humiliated Shonga as he stood up.

'Now, listen carefully. I want your little church nicely cleaned. Then I want some mats laid out—How many mats, boy?'

'Twenty-two, Boss.'

'That's the boy! I want each mat as far away from the others as possible. Understand?'

'Yes, Boss.'

'We are all very hungry. You know how hard we work. Now I want you to slaughter a nice fat ox. I want you to roast the meat like you used to do at the mine. When it's ready, you are to bring it inside the church. OK?'

Shonga did not reply.

'I said do you understand?'

'Yes—Boss.'

'Before you go and slaughter the ox—In fact, I want you to do that now. Tell all the men that they are dismissed. They must go back to their huts . . . Come on, tell them now!'

'Boss says all the men go to their huts now!' Shonga shouted. A buzz of grumbling whispers went up as the men left for their huts.

'Tell them to hurry up!'

'Boss wants you to hurry up!'

Soon all the men were gone.

'Now tell all the old women to get back to their huts!'

Shonga told the old women to go home.

'Now you can go and slaughter the ox. I will take care of the rest myself.'

'No, Boss.'

'What did you say, boy?!'

'I said no, Boss.'

Suddenly Hill tried to grab Shonga. But Shonga started running away. The rest of the women, who were now very terrified, also started running away from the white men. Hill chased Shonga shouting at him to stop. But Shonga kept on running. Hill took out his gun and fired one shot just above Shonga's head. That stopped Shonga.

'Fire some shots above the heads of those beasts!' Hill shouted to his men.

A volley rang through the air. But this only made the girls and the women run faster. It took the noise of the volley to wake Mills. He came out of his hut. After his eyes were used to the brightness of day-light, he looked at the church and saw Hill still pointing a gun at Shonga. Mills hurried over to the church.

'Hill! For heaven's sake, put that thing away! What do you think you are doing?'

'What's up, old chap? You told us you were leaving for Chuma's village yesterday? Nigger boy here too, told us you left yesterday. What's up? Have you got something to hide? Tell us! No need to be ashamed about having a little affair with a nigger girl!' taunted Hill.

'Are you out of your mind, Hill? . . . Oh! you are drunk—' said Mills as he came closer to Hill.

'Now listen to me, Mills. Drunk or sober, that's not material. When you first arrived here, you were ill and desperate. We did everything we could for you. Last week Simpson and his gang arrived here. And what do you do? You tell them everything about the diamond deposits at Chuma's village. I have seen you twice since you saw last Simpson. But you decided not to tell me a thing about it! You dream up this story of going to open a mission at Chuma's village, and don't go. Lies and lies is all we get from you!'

'What's all this nonsense about Simpson?'

'Who could have guessed that I would live to see the day when a priest would tell me lies!'

'Look, Hill I did go to Chuma's village! Now, what's all this diamond deposits business about?'

'I can understand the natives lying. They are born with it. But you! Anyway, we now know everything we want to know about the diamond deposits at Chuma's. You and your boy are going to do us a good turn for a change. I must say I admire you, Mills; you are pretty good at taming the natives.

You are going to give us a hand! Today! Now!'

'I—we shall do no such a thing. I have only just arrived
from Chuma's village early this morning. It's no good. There
is bound to be violence.'

'I know they are cheeky bastards. But we are going to teach
them a lesson. You will see when we get there!'

'Hill, we are not going.'

'Listen, old man, you wouldn't like your superiors to know
about some of the things you have been up to here. Would
you?'

'What on earth are you trying to suggest, Hill?'

'I am not suggesting anything. Are you coming with us or
not?'

'No!'

'All right. You win. We can't force you. But nigger boy
here, your "assistant" as you like to call him, certainly is.
After all, I brought him from there. Now, I want to take him
back!'

That young man, Shonga suffered much at the hands of
Hill and his men. They beat him; they tied his hands and let
a horse drag him some of the way to Chuma's village. They
didn't let him drink any water or have any food. They tied him
to a tree and shot at the tree all round him. One of the white
men missed and shot Shonga in the palm. Finally, the spirits
of the ancestors came to his rescue. Nobody knows quite what
happened. Shonga got some strength from somewhere. As
they continued the journey to Chuma's he broke loose and ran
like a wild animal. Hill and his men and their tired horses
tried to pursue him but Shonga was not following the track.
He ran through the bush. When he arrived at Chief Chuma's
huts, he told the Chief to sound the war drum. After the
warriors had gathered, Chief Chuma sent them to go and
meet the white men. But the white men did not arrive. All the
same, Chief Chuma decided to keep his warriors deployed
around the village. After some days, the warriors were put off
the alert. The white men must have returned to Mtoko after
Shonga's escape.

Shonga began to settle down in the village. Many people
gathered every evening to hear the stories about his life with

the white men at Mtoko's village. He told them how Chief Mtoko had lost dignity and the respect of his people because of Hill and Mills. He spoke about how he and Mills had started the mission at Mtoko. They had started by getting to know the people in the village. Mills had given many garments and other presents to Chief Mtoko and his elders. Chief Mtoko allowed Mills to open a mission. Every Sunday, Mills preached about his God. Shonga had done the translating. People used to come to Shonga and tell him that he translated the preaching like a possessed man. To begin with, many people had found this very entertaining. They had also been fascinated by Mills' appearance. But after some time, most people became bored. However, a few had begun to believe in what Mills preached.

There was one Sunday when Mills had devoted his sermon to attacking witch doctors, witches, and the worship of the spirits of the ancestors. He branded them all as evil. Not surprisingly, many people at Mtoko's village were very angered by this attack. One witch was so angry that she publicly threatened Mills. She told him that unless he and Shonga left Mtoko's village within three days, they would 'see' what was going to happen. Shonga himself had been very frightened; but Mills had assured him that 'the power of God would not let any such evil befall' them. Three days after the witch's threat, Shonga and Mills were sitting down to their evening meal. It began to rain and thunder. After several flashes of lightning, the two men were thrown out of their hut. All their three huts and belongings had been totally gutted by fire.

By chance, the day after the lightning had destroyed their huts, Mills was visited by a group of white mineral hunters. At that time, the villagers were not yet used to seeing many white men. When Mtoko's people saw the group of whites, they believed that Mills' God had sent them to punish the people of the village for what the witch had done to Mills. So they fled into the bush when the white men arrived. But they came back after assuring themselves that the white men had left. Really it was from that day that Chief Mtoko began to lose his authority because he had told his people to try and follow 'whatever it is' that Mills preached.

   One night, a month or so after Shonga's return to Chuma's
village, Hill and his men made a surprise attack on the
village. They did not use their guns until after they had set fire
to many huts. Most people were asleep inside huts and they
burned to death. Others tried to escape but that was when
Hill and his men used their guns. They shot anybody who was
trying to escape. Some of the warriors managed to arm
themselves and fought very fiercely. The white men finally
retreated. When the sun rose the next morning, people
counted the dead. They also found some corpses of white
men. Shonga was one of those who had been killed. They
found him with his fingers still clawed around the neck of a
white man. He too was dead . . .

'That's the end of the story. What I want you to know is that
this is a true story. It took place here in our village and
Mtoko's village. Chief Chuma was really Chief Makosa, the
grandfather of our present Chief Makosa. The man called
Shonga was the elder brother of my father. The man I called
Rev Mills is your Rev Cope. He has now lived in our village
for many years. He came to live here soon after the story I
have just told you took place.'

'Why was he not killed when he came to Makosa?' a small
boy would ask.

'Well, because he didn't come alone . . . About one week
after the night battle I have just told you about, although Hill
had been killed—'

'—Was he killed by Shonga?'

'No one knows for certain who actually killed Hill. Some
say it was Shonga, others say it was this or that
warrior . . . Anyway, after that battle, the white men who had
retreated returned to our village. More of our people,
including the then Chief Makosa, were killed. It is said if it
had not been for Rev Cope, everyone in the village would have
been killed. Hill's men spent four months in our village but
left when they failed to find the diamonds they had hoped to
find outside the village. Rev Cope asked the new Chief
Makosa to be allowed to stay. The Chief agreed. The result of
his long stay is your school, your church and your medicine-

house. And for me children like Rugare, and grand-children like you. What are you learning? To lose your traditional ways. And what will you be after that?

. . . Except for the names, everything I have told you tonight is true.'

The children would ask a few more questions after stories such as this. Sekuru would allow a few before sending the children to their huts to sleep as it would be long after midnight. Sekuru had told many stories about tribal wars, locust invasions, years of famine and other legendary stories.

BOOK TWO: DISCOVERING THE TIME

THERE WAS NOTHING particularly unusual about the fact that at the same time Sekuru was so ill, one of his daughters-in-law, Tendayi, the wife of Rugare, the old man's only son with his late third wife, was pregnant. This was her fourth pregnancy. Unfortunately, the other three pregnancies had all ended as miscarriages. Everyone in the village was hoping this time she would have the baby.

Tendayi's family home was at Mtoko's village. She had first come to Makosa in order to visit her childhood friend and niece, Shupi. Shupi was married to a man from Makosa. It was during this visit that Tendayi and Rugare first met. Rugare was a good friend of Shupi's husband. Rugare had courted Tendayi. A few days before Tendayi was to return home to Mtoko, Rugare had proposed marriage to her. Although she had known that she loved Rugare and wanted to be his wife, Tendayi had not immediately consented to marrying him. In those days, it was patience and persistence that proved whether a man loved a woman or not. Rugare had been very persistent. On the day she left for Mtoko, Tendayi had consented to marrying Rugare. But it had been one long year before any marriage formalities began.

This is what had happened. The marriage formalities began one evening when a man named Chimusoro arrived at Tendayi's home. He was the man Rugare and his father Sekuru, had chosen to be the middle-man. Chimusoro was a very artful middle-man. Without much difficulty and without making any blunders, he sought and got the consideration of Rugare as a possible husband for Tendayi from her father. Soon after Chimusoro had left for Makosa, Rugare arrived at Mtoko for the customary 'stay'. During his 'stay', Rugare built a new and larger cattle pen, and trained a couple of oxen for ploughing. He rethatched five of the family's nine huts and also cut down trees and cleared bushes over a substantial area of ground in an effort to extend the family's field. Rugare had performed all these tasks not only diligently but competently as well. Tendayi's father was impressed and full of admiration. As Rugare returned home to Makosa, it was Chimusoro's turn to be at Mtoko. Knowing that his client had accomplished his tasks very well, Chimusoro confidently set

about the talks on *roora*. He respectfully talked Tendayi's
father down to a low number of cattle. In a day or two, *roora*,
in the sum of seven oxen and five cows, was amicably agreed
upon. Within a month of the agreement, the animals were
delivered to Tendayi's father. It was also on the same day that
Tendayi chose her youngest sister to be the traditional maid of
the bride.

Finally, Rugare arrived at Mtoko again to take his wife
home. He arrived one late afternoon and stayed overnight.
Tendayi and her maid had spent most of that day saying
goodbye to friends, village elders and their family. She and
her maid spent the evening packing her personal belongings
and her marriage presents. The marriage presents included
an assortment of clay-pot, wooden plates and bowls, straw
chaff-separators, a variety of seeds and a smoked leg of
wildebeeste. These presents and personal belongings were
packed in two large rush-baskets which were then covered
with pieces of cloth.

At the third crow of the cock, the party was on its way to
Makosa's village. Shouldering a roll of reed-mats—another
marriage present—Rugare led the way. The two women,
carrying the bundled baskets on their heads, followed closely
behind. They covered much ground in the early morning but
as the sun rose higher and got hotter, their pace slackened.
After walking for six hours, they arrived at Makosa. A lavish
welcoming celebration awaited the new bride. Rugare's family
had slaughtered an ox and brewed some beer. Everyone in the
village had been invited. For two days, there was much
singing, dancing and feasting at Sekuru's huts.

As soon as the celebration was over, Tendayi, with the
assistance of her maid, began her traditional duties as a new
bride as well as settle in her new home. Her marriage had
taken place in the middle of the autumn. She and her
husband had many things to do.

Like most young men in the village, Rugare had not begun
the autumn by taking a rest. He had built two huts, one to be
used as a kitchen and the other for sleeping. He had
completed the building of these huts before Tendayi arrived.
Also before he went to bring his wife home, he had gone to the

granite hills, searched and brought home four large and suitable stones for his grain-house to sit on. He had gathered poles, twigs, bark-rope and thatch. Now he had just finished building the grain-house.

After reporting his marriage plans to Chief Makosa, Rugare had been allocated a piece of land for his field. He was now clearing bushes on that piece of land for his field. Apart from the twelve cattle for *roora,* Rugare had received another two oxen, three cows and one calf from his father. Only one ox was good to plough with. He would need to break the second one. Before he could do that, he would need to make at least two yokes and a couple of pairs of animal-skin strips. Sekuru had also given his son an old plough but it did not have a chain to link it to a yoke. Rugare and Tendayi would have to spend many of their evenings cracking groundnuts to exchange for a chain at 'Boss' Kaplan's store.

There were jobs connected with next ploughing and sowing season, the following weeding period and the subsequent harvest which needed doing before the autumn was over. Rugare, an ardent hunter and a skilled drum maker did not mind foregoing these pastimes this autumn.

Daily, Tendayi got up before sunrise. She began the day by pounding grain in a mortar with a pestle. She would leave the pounded grain in a chaff-separator to be dried by the rising sun. Next, she took her mother-in-law's dirty utensils and her own down to the village-well where she cleaned them. Back at the huts, she would light the fire and warm some water before making several trips to the village-well in order to refill the clay water pitchers. Starting with Sekuru and following a descending order of seniority, she offered all the members of the family the warm water to wash their hands and faces. The new bride would boil some cassava-roots, or yams or make porridge for everyone's breakfast. After breakfast, it would be time to clean and tidy the huts. On some days, she worked in the vegetable patch near the huts; on others, she would kneel down at the grindstone, and perhaps humming a love tune, she would grind the grain into a soft and fine flour. If a villager dropped by, she disappeared into the kitchen and came out with a gourdful of clay-tasting milky water. She would kneel down and respectfully offer the visitor the water. Then, humbly, she greeted the visitor before withdrawing to her grindstone. A quick glance at the sun would tell her it was time to start preparing the midday meal. When lunch was done with, she would learn something of the local gossip and back-biting while plaiting the hair of any one of the womenfolk in the family, or maybe one of her new friends in the village. In the cooler late afternoon, together with other women, she went wood-gathering or down to the river to wash rags and loin-cloths and bathe. By the time she got back home, she would have just enough time to make the last trip of the day to the village-well to wash the midday meal dishes before preparing the evening meal.

Eventually, Tendayi's term of duty as a new bride elapsed. This only meant she did not have to do things for Rugare's whole family. The family, neighbours and other villagers expressed much satisfaction with Rugare's wife. She was a hard-working, cheerful and a very respectful young woman. This also marked the end of her sister's duty as a maid. Before Tandayi's sister returned to Mtoko, Rugare took her to 'Boss' Kaplan's store where they exchanged some maize for a dress. The girl had chosen a plain yellow frock. A day or so later, Rugare accompanied the girl back to Mtoko.

On the day Rugare returned from Mtoko, by chance he met Rev Cope on the path in the village. After greeting each other, the Rev wondered if, for a few garments and a small amount of money, Rugare would rethatch the church in the village. Rugare readily agreed. Soon, Rugare began work on the church. A very close friendship between Rev Cope and Rugare began to develop. This led to Rugare and his wife being converted to the Christian faith. In turn, Rugare and Tendayi's conversion led to the beginning of a series of quarrels with the rest of his family. While all this was going on, for the first time, Tendayi got pregnant.

When the first miscarriage took place, Tendayi did not go to Sekuru for help. As Christians, they regarded witches, medicine-men and the worship of the spirits of the ancestors as 'evil'. So they had simply prayed and prayed for a child who would live. But after two more miscarriages, they found that

their Lord was not answering their prayers. Rugare became
disillusioned with Christianity and began contemplating
taking a second wife. But Tendayi pleaded that they should
ask for Sekuru's help first.

So, after the third miscarriage, they had visited Sekuru. It
was early in the morning, an hour or so after sunrise. Tendayi
and Rugare came out of their sleeping-hut and walked the few
paces to Sekuru's hut. From the smoke that issued through
the damp roof-thatch of his hut and the coughing that could
be heard coming out of it, they knew that Sekuru was already
awake.

Clearing his throat, Rugare pushed open the door and they
entered. They sat down before the fire in front of the old man.
After bidding him good-morning, there followed a com-
municative silence. They were there for help. Sekuru understood. Then he began by saying:

'After all this time . . . After all these tragedies, today you
finally come to me. Tell me . . . Why? . . . I know you did not
come before because you are Christians and you do not believe
in medicine-men. What has changed now? . . . What is it that
has changed?'

'Father,' responded Rugare in a humble but earnest voice,
'mistakes have been made. We have done many wrong things.
I beg you, with all your kindness, to forgive us. We needn't
tell you why we are here. You know everything—everything we
have been through. Especially your daughter-in-law here.
Please forgive us.'

'And the white man, your friend . . . he can't help you?'
Sekuru asked with sharp bitterness.

Neither Rugare nor his wife dared to reply.

'You finally decided: "Why not give it a try", eh? You and
your white man friend believe medicine-men are "evil". You
have forsaken most of our customs and traditions because you
think you are modern people! . . . I say you are no modern
people! You are not even enlightened as you wish to believe!
All you do is hunger for that white man's garments! His
money! His way of life! . . . You want to live like white people.
You can try as long as you like, but you will never succeed . . .
What you must learn is this. Truly modern people come out of

traditions . . . their established customs and their way of life. Do you hear me, Rugare?'

'I hear you, father.'

'If you don't want to believe what I say, you can ask your friend, the white man. He is the only one you believe now. He will tell you I speak the truth.'

'Father-in-law—'

'I speak to you as your father, Rugare. Not as a medicine-man. You hear?'

'Indeed, father.'

'Father-in-law,' Tendayi began again, her voice as gentle and as respectful as it could be, 'I too, beg for your forgiveness. Both Rugare and I feel much shame. Not only in front of you. But also in the eyes of the rest of the people in this village. We came to *you* because you can help us. You are the only one who can help us. If we did not believe in *you*, you would have known it even before we came. I know that's part of the powers you have. That white man and his church are now behind us. Please, and I touch my knees, forgive us. Help us.'

'Father, we shall do anything—anything at all that you and the spirits of the ancestors shall require of us. Please—' appealed Rugare.

'I hear you . . . Yes. I hear you, my children. You must now listen to what I have to say,' Sekuru said in a softer tone of voice.

'After the first tragedy, I waited for you to come. But you did not come . . . I was saddened. Both by the miscarriage and your not coming to me . . . I waited—I was anxious to find out why such a misfortune had to happen in my family. Of course there was nothing I could do by myself. As you should know, a medicine-man of our totem *can not* initiate consultations with the spirits of the ancestors without a request from someone. This is especially so when the need for consultations concerns someone in the family . . . Again after the second tragedy, I waited but as you know, you never came. I could not bear it. How could I just sit here and watch tragedy after tragedy? I came and tried to talk to you, Rugare. But you shunned me . . . my own child! . . . my blood! . . . In my sorrow and frustration—Of course, I knew I would be punished for it. One evening, I just decided and consulted them. At first, they showed me everything. Everything I wanted to know . . . Then, they informed me how angry they were. Indeed, they are still very angry with me.'

'What is to be done, father?'

'. . . to be done? . . . Oh, to have your child?'

'Well . . . Y-yes, to have children, father.'

'You see, it's my mother. Your grandmother. You were her favourite grandchild, do you still remember?'

'I remember well, father.'

'Her spirit is troubled. I did not know this before. It was revealed to me by the spirits of the ancestors. But when she died, mother was mourned and buried in accordance with *our* totem rites and *not* those of her family. She wants this put right. The onus happens to fall on you, Rugare. She wants you to slaughter a black cow—completely spotless—and brew some beer. You are to ask Nungo, the present head of the family of our traditional joking-friends to come and preside over the offering ceremony. After that, the spirits of the ancestors shall bless you with a child. A son.'

'Father-in-law, I am very grateful indeed. But you keep on saying: "child"?'

'Tendayi, daughter-in-law, I can only tell you what the spirits of the ancestors showed me. How many children you will have entirely depends on you and Rugare's conduct. Need I tell you about the bad words on the tongues of many people in the village about you both? The spirits of the ancestors are already aware of this. They are not pleased, Rugare . . . You can't go on defying their will any longer. You have to mend your ways. Take this as a warning. If you persist, my child, they are going to take you . . . I saw it quite clearly . . . They will take you without any hesitation.'

'How soon can we hold the offering ceremony, father?'

'You will not find that black cow easily, Rugare. And remember, it must be totally black. Just as soon as you find it, hold the ceremony . . . Your son and I shall—No. I shall not say that . . . No,' said the old man as he sadly and slowly shook his head.

Most of those who were present say the baby was born soon after the old man, his grandfather, died. Yes, on the very same day. In fact, a few people go so far as to swear the shadow of the body had just disappeared when the first cry of the new baby was heard. Of course, people recount the story with varying versions and different interpretations. However, they all tend to agree about one thing: there had to be something more than a mere coincidence between Sekuru's death and the birth of the child on that same day.

Rugare and Tendayi had chosen a name for their child a few months before he was born. Although Sekuru had foretold them the baby would be a boy, they had not really believed him. Instead, they had taken the small precaution of choosing both a girl's name and a boy's name. They would name a girl Chipo—meaning a gift; and to a boy, they would give the name Chikomborero, which means a blessing. As far as they were concerned, any child they would have was a blessing from the spirits of the ancestors. When the baby boy was born, for short, everyone affectionately called him Chiko. For a time, Rugare, his wife and child lived very happily and showed much gratitude to the spirits of the ancestors.

But when Chiko was nearly two years old, the Rev Cope, the elderly British Methodist missionary who had been living in Makosa's village for many years, succeeded in reconverting the boy's parents to the Christian religion. They had lost their faith at the time of their visit to Rugare's late father. Soon after this reconversion Chiko was baptized. At the christening, the 'pagan' name Chiko was dropped for the new and 'civilized' name Alexio. It took some time for relatives and other villagers to get used to addressing Chiko as Alexio. But after a few months everyone was calling him Alexio. In contrast, no one bothered to address Tendayi as Ma Alexio instead of Ma Chiko or Rugare, Baba wa Alexio instead of Baba wa Chiko. People simply continued to call them Ma Chiko and Baba wa Chiko.

Alexio remembered being quite confused about the change of his name from Chiko to Alexio. He had known that he was Chiko. But then, why were people now calling him Alexio? If he was Alexio, then why did people address his parents by Chiko's name?

Another early memory Alexio recalled was of a journey he had with his father. Strangely enough he could not remember whether they were travelling from Makosa's village to his mother's family home at Mtoko or vice versa. He was, however, certain they had been somewhere between the two villages. All he recollected was that they were at a mountain pass. Alexio was securely shawled up on to his father's back. The path they followed took them over the mountain pass. It was a narrow path with many turns and twists to avoid the many rocks that beset it. The sky at the mountain pass had been padded with dark clouds. The tall, thin and leafy trees under which the path passed had made the mountain pass a very dark and desolately gloomy place. Alexio recalled bursting into a cry but not the reason for it. He surmised that it could have been because of the gloom he felt; or that he might have cried simply because he was hungry or thirsty or both. Anyway, his father had released him from the shawl and placed a gourd on his lips. From it, Alexio had greedily gulped some milk. Then his father had cajoled him into trying to urinate before they continued with their journey. The little man had tried and tried but had failed. Understandably, Alexio had wanted to stretch his legs with a little walk down the hill. But downhill or uphill, his father hadn't let him. Perhaps there hadn't been enough time for short walks which took a long time. His father had playfully piggy-backed him on to his back again and continued walking up the pass. Alexio had protested in the one way he knew: he howled when, in fact, he wasn't crying at all. His father had merely ignored him.

This was probably Alexio's earliest memory. It was also his only vivid memory of his father. Sometime soon after this journey, his parents were weeding in a part of their field. They left Alexio alone to play under a Msasa-tree which stood in the middle of the field. Although there were scattered clouds in the sky, most of the day was hot and dry. However, in the late afternoon, dark clouds of rain had drifted over and stationed themselves over the face of the sun. Thunder roared several times. A tropical shower began falling. Ma Chiko and Baba wa Chiko hurried to take shelter under the Msasa-tree. But when they got there, their child wasn't playing alone. A medium-sized black snake was coiled around the child. It was licking Alexio's face with its fangs. The boy was laughing and warding off the snake's kisses with his short chubby arms. In her shock, Ma Chiko screamed before she froze silent with fear. The snake uncoiled. In interposed itself between them and Chiko. The child began to cry.

Baba wa Chiko rushed from behind the snake and snatched the child away. While Ma Chiko looked for any snake-bites all over her naked child's body and wiped off what she believed to be the poisonous saliva of the snake, the snake slowly began moving towards a thicket at the edge of the field. Armed with an axe Baba wa Chiko pursued the black snake. As he tried to kill it, a flash of lightning tore the sky. It was a blinding flash. When she recovered from being blinded Ma Chiko looked around and saw her husband. He was lying still on the ground and getting drenched by the falling rain. She rushed to him and then she became totally hysterical. He was dead. She screamed and screamed. By and by, a number of the villagers who heard her screams from their own fields, arrived. They carried Rugare's charred remains back to the village. A death of this nature was not of frequent occurrence in Makosa's village. As the news of Rugare's death spread, the whole village became stunned. Rugare was mourned and buried. But Tendayi could not stop mourning.

It was now almost a year since they had buried her husband. But, Ma Chiko was still mourning as intensely as if he had died only the previous week. She had not seen the path that led to the fields since the day they had carried Rugare's body from there. She had ceased attending church services. She had told Rev Cope and all her friends to leave her alone. She shunned virtually everybody. She never went out of her hut unless she had to. She had nothing much to do inside her hut. She simply sat in silence most of the time. She fed Alexio when she remembered to or when he cried. She herself ate barely enough to keep body and soul together. Besides losing much weight, Ma Chiko had become very aged since the death of her husband.

The only regular visitor she now had was Gomo, her late husband's eldest step-brother. Gomo had become head of the whole extended family after Sekuru's death. Traditionally, all responsibility over Rugare's child and widow fell on Gomo. Therefore, two and sometimes three times a week, Gomo stopped by Ma Chiko's hut to find out how she and the child were. Gomo had found the once-cheerful woman inconsolable, aloof, and at times even bitter. He had been patient and kind with her. He knew what she had gone through since she had arrived at Makosa as his step-brother's new bride. But after a year since Rugare's death without much change, Gomo felt she had mourned for far too long. He had given her more than enough time. He could wait no longer.

In order to give weight to his scheme, Gomo decided not to visit Ma Chiko for some two weeks. But right away, Ma Chiko knew what this meant. Without any doubt, she also knew what she was going to do. Her resolution gave her a little more strength in her spirit. On the day Gomo was to come to her hut, although she did not know this, she cleaned and tidied her hut. For the first time in weeks, she bathed and fed her child properly. She also accomplished other general household chores. When she finished, she lit a fire and sat, cross-legged, before it.

Consciously or unconsciously, it was difficult to determine. But Ma Chiko had piled a little too much wood on her fire. The little hut became filled by a thick cloud of smoke. When the fire began burning properly, high flames, particularly for such a small hut, leapt up dangerously close to the roof-thatch. Apart from coughing because of the smoke and sweating because of the heat, Ma Chiko remained very calm and unperturbed. Soon, however, much of the smoke seeped out through the roof-thatch and through the small partially open entrance to the hut. The high flames eventually subsided.

In the glow of the fire, Ma Chiko's face revealed the extent of her anguish. It was deep anguish.

'If he walks in this moment, I shall just say it was the smoke,' she thought to herself as tears mingled with sweat rolled down her dark face. Through the tears which drowned her still keen brown eyes, she gazed into the fire. After a while, she tried to focus her eyes on her little boy. But she only just then sensed that her tears were raining on his naked body. Wearing only half smile on his face, Alexio remained fast asleep on her lap. She wiped the tear drops off with her bare and rough hand. She then rubbed dry her own face before contemplating him. Her eyes implored him for something—something she knew he could not even understand. A wave of pain came over her face before she sighed a sigh of tiredness.

'I don't think I am in my right mind,' she thought again. But there and then, her mind began to wander back in time. Silently, she visualized her whole life once again as she had done many times in the last year.

The sound of the heavy gait was unmistakable. When she heard it, Ma Chiko's heart began pounding in unison. Gomo entered into the hut and sat down. They exchanged polite greetings: Gomo asking how Alexio was and Ma Chiko after the health of Gomo's two wives, Ma Rudo and Ma Sekayi and all their children. After this, the expected serious talk began.

'You know, Ma Chiko, your husband was my relative too—my brother. It is still hard for all of us. But how long can you go on like this? You can't go on doing this to yourself and to the child.'

Gomo was trying to be as gentle as he could be.

'Gomo, sire, as you can see, I do not have much strength left in me. Please, don't beat about the bush. Let's come to the point,' Ma Chiko quivered.

'Well, we shall. Don't you think your mourning has gone on for a little too long? People in the village are now beginning to wonder whether you are really still mourning or you are now sulking for some other reason. As I said at the beginning, he was my brother as well. But life must go on. We have this little man here to think about. What do you say, my dear woman?'

'Sire, what do you want me to do?' asked Ma Chiko in the same tense voice.

'Listen to me, my woman. It's not just what I want you to do. It's what tradition lays down. I am not in a hurry to come into your hut. That can wait until the wounds of the heart have healed. But I think you ought to make a start on all your other wifely duties. You still have your field, you know. Ma Rudo and Ma Sekayi can't go on working on it for you. They have their own fields. I am not too worried about what you want to do with yourself; but you can't bring up the child in this way. I am not the only one concerned. The whole village is talking. It's as if you don't care about this child. What do you say, Ma Chiko?'

'Sire, it is true that by tradition you are now my husband. But could you not let me leave for Mtoko and let me bring up your child? Again, I know tradition says—'

'I see! This is why. Well, if you can't look after the child here, how will you be able to look after him any better at Mtoko? Unless you have your eyes on another man already, I don't see why you want to leave Makosa.'

'There is no other man, Gomo sire. I don't want another man. I can't—it's impossible.'

'I have just told you. I am not in a hurry to come into your hut. All I want you to do is to pull yourself together, look after the child in a reasonable manner and lead as normal a life as you can . . . Is that much to ask, Ma Chiko?'

'Gomo, today, tomorrow or ten years from now, I don't want another man in my life. You are not going to inherit me! I am telling you: all I want is to bring up this child.'

'Tendayi, you are still young. You can say what you like about never wanting another man. But in six months from now, it will be a different story. Now, if you don't want to be my wife, of course the proper thing is for you to go back to your family home. But I can't let you take the child. Even if I wanted to. You know very well what would happen to me, don't you?'

'I beg you, Gomo. When your boy here is of age, I have no reason to keep him. He will be a man anyway; he will want to be with his people. If I left for my home, who would bring him up?'

'Tendayi! I am not going to be like Rugare whom you told

what to do! He would probably be alive today if—if he had listened to you less—'

'You dog! You are saying I killed my husband! You were pleased when he died because you thought you would have me, weren't you? For as long as I live, I could never be your wife! You are a dog—'

'Shut up!' shouted Gomo as he slapped her on the cheeks quite a few times.

'You have no respect for a man! You are a snake! Your head is full of water and that white man's ideas. It was your desire for garments and money that killed my brother! How can I let you bring up this child? You will ruin him! I say No! Now, listen to me. Tomorrow! This tomorrow! You leave for your home! That's final!'

Tendayi was crying. Gomo stood up and snatched the baby from her lap and stormed out of the hut. The child had been crying since the shouting began, but now he was screaming with a bitterness that chokes at the throat.

Gomo, who had hoped that one of his wives would look after the child, found himself with the serious problem of finding someone else to mind the boy. Both his wives refused to take charge of the child even on a temporary basis. They offered to be divorced rather than mind that child. Finally, Gomo had to place the child with his aging mother.

Gomo's eldest child was a girl called Rudo. A few years before, Rudo had left the village to go and find a job in Salisbury. She had done this mainly to help her father pay the newly introduced taxes. She was an obedient and somewhat docile girl. Initially, Rudo had hoped to work only a few months and then return home. But, as time went by, she discovered that she had settled in Salisbury permanently. She kept in touch with her family. At the end of each month, she always sent a small parcel to her family. Sometimes it was a few old shirts or pairs of trousers for her father, brothers and uncles. At other times, it was second-hand skirts, dresses, sweaters and blouses and shawls for the womenfolk. Whenever she could spare some money, she sent some to her father.

It was after Gomo had received a small parcel from his

daughter that it occurred to him that she might be able to help with the problem of Alexio. Immediately, he sent word about his plight to her. In time, Rudo sent back word that she would have Alexio.

On an agreed day, Gomo took Alexio to where the bus usually stopped in the centre of the village—at Boss Kaplan's store. When the bus arrived, Gomo, carrying Alexio in his arms, edged his way through the usual crowd of villagers who came to watch the bus. When Gomo handed Alexio over to the bus conductor, the latter complained about the appearance of the child.

'Knowing that he is going to Salisbury, for once in his life, couldn't you have bathed him or just given him a wash?'

Alexio's hair was matted with dust. His cheeks were decorated with several tracks of dried salty tears. His lips were white with hunger or thirst. A few flies hovered over the mucus on his runny nose. He was only clad in a tattered over-sized khaki shirt which was grey with dirt.

'Doesn't he have any bag, or something to carry?'

Gomo shook his head. At that moment, Ma Rudo arrived at the bus stop.

'Gomo, sire, where are you sending this child?' she asked nervously.

'Where do you think I am sending him to?'

'I am only asking. I hope you are not sending him to Rudo that's all.'

She got her reply from the conductor.

'You just want me to give the boy to Rudo.—No message or anything like that?' he asked loudly.

'Sire, how can you do that to your own daughter? Is that your way of showing your gratitude to her for all she has done for you? You know this child is . . . Even if he was a normal child, you know Rudo has to work. How could she look after a child and work—?'

Gomo felt very embarrassed.

'Why didn't you tell me about it before? I am not going to let that child go to Rudo—No!'

The bus pulled off. Alexio was not quite sure what was happening. He had never been in a bus before. He was a little frightened but didn't cry. A woman who was sitting near the front end of the bus offered to take care of the child on the journey. Alexio slept on the greater part of the journey. When the bus arrived at Harare Market, Rudo was there waiting for him. On being handed over to another unfamiliar face, Alexio cried.

Rudo worked in the white suburb of Highlands. Her employer, Mrs van der Byl, was a widow. Her husband, a pilot in the Royal Air Force, had died towards the end of the Second World War. Mrs van der Byl and her twin sons, Peter and John, lived in a seven-roomed bungalow.

Rudo had been very fortunate. Within two days of her arrival in Salisbury, she had found a job. On the day she arrived, she went to stay with a distant uncle, a man named Shiri, who lived in the Magaba section of Harare township. This arrangement had been made for Rudo by her father, Gomo, before she left Makosa's village. Shiri explained to Rudo how difficult it was to find any job in Salisbury. It was more difficult to find jobs in the suburbs nearer to Harare. However, he advised her to go to a suburb like Highlands, twelve to thirteen miles from Harare, on the other side of the city. She would have a better chance of getting a job there.

Shiri had to warn Rudo about many things.

'You should always look on both sides of the road before you cross. Buses, cars and bicycles don't stop for pedestrians except at traffic lights in the city. You should always cross when other people are crossing. But in the city people are dangerous too. There are many *tsotsis* (pick-pockets). Never keep your money in your dress-pockets. Some *tsotsis* can tell you they are going to help you find a job; then they will lead you somewhere quiet and rob you. So be careful to whom you talk.'

Shiri told Rudo about many other dangers of life in the city. The next morning before she left for Highlands, Shiri gave her directions to get there. Highlands was on the main road to Mtoko. He added:

'Its a long walk from here. But as I told you, you will have a better chance there. Don't forget what I have told you. White people don't like you to arrive at their houses by the front

entrance. They can get you arrested for that; or they can set
dogs on you. Approach houses from the rear. Don't walk into
a yard until someone sees you. Stick to the sanitary lanes. You
understand me? . . . Well, I hope everything will go well for
you. If you can't find a job today, come back home. But don't
lose heart. We may see you here tonight. And if you get a job,
let us know where you are. Good luck!'

Rudo had walked from Magaba, through the city and out
to Highlands. It took her a long time to get to Highlands. This
was partly because of the distance and partly because of sightseeing. Just about everything she saw was new to her. Between
Magaba and the city, everyone was black. All the people she
saw were very different from the people at Makosa. City
people! The way they walked and carried themselves! Their
way of speaking! Their language! Their clothes! Rudo felt
ashamed in her simple straight dress. She wanted to take off
her calico head-scarf and throw it away. No! She didn't have
to wear a head-scarf! Look at all those women! They had no
scarves. Their hair was neatly combed. But she couldn't take
that scarf off because her hair was plaited. That was even
more shameful. She would buy herself one of those colourful
berets or a beautiful head-scarf like some of the women were
wearing with her first pay! That was a promise!

Would she really be able to live in a place like that? So
many people! Bicycles! Not to talk about cars! To think she
would soon get used to it all! Yes. She would be one of them
soon. The job. If only the spirits of the ancestors could help
her get that job!

When she came near the city, she had to concentrate. There
were too many cars, too many buses, too many bicycles, too
many people! The people! They made her nervous. How could
each one know where they were going? She was sure some of
them were *tsotsis*. She had to be careful. The best thing was to
behave like one of them. Dressed like that? With her gait?
Everybody knew she was a girl from a 'Reserve', she thought.
She felt as if it was written all over her and disliked the
feeling.

Then she saw a 'real' white man. Rev Cope and the whites
who visited him at Makosa were not 'real' white men

anymore—because they they ate *sadza*. She couldn't take her
eyes off the 'real' white man. Thud! She bumped into
someone. She should look where she was going! She
apologized. She promised herself she wouldn't stare at any
more white people. After all they were just people. As she
proceeded deeper into the city, there were more and more
white people. If only people at Makosa knew where she was!
There were even more cars. The buildings! Their colours!
Their heights! The shops! They all sailed past her. The things
inside the shops! Rudo was amazed by everything she saw.

When she began to leave the city behind her, she noticed a
change. There were no more crowds. There were fewer and
fewer black people. She saw more white people. This change
began to frighten her. But she kept on walking. Then she
looked all around her. Not a black man in sight! Only white
people. In front of her. Behind her. All round her. Something
was wrong! Could she be lost? She stopped. She was now very
frightened. She turned round and hurried towards the city.
But then she saw a black man walking towards her. She felt as
if he had saved her from some great danger. She wanted to
talk to him. She had to say something to him. But what could
she say? She had been warned against talking to strangers. He
looked like a *tsotsi*. They passed each other. She didn't say
anything. She kept on walking but turning to look at the man.
She stopped and turned round. She decided to follow him.
She would keep her distance. If anything was going to happen
she could shout and he would hear her. She hoped he would
not turn off before she got to Highlands.

She saw a white woman with two children walking towards
her. Her heart began to beat. What was she going to do? If
she didn't greet the white woman and her children, they might
think she was rude. That could mean trouble. She should
greet them. Maybe if Rudo greeted the white woman nicely,
she might even be offered a job. As the white woman and the
children came nearer, Rudo moved to the edge of the curb.
She half knelt with her hands clasped together and said:

'Good morning, Madam.' The white woman and her
children did not answer. It was as if Rudo did not exist. Rudo
felt very degraded. After this, she decided to reduce the dis-

tance between herself and the black man ahead of her. There were two more white people, a man and a woman, coming towards her. She was going to watch what the black man in front of her did. The man had an old straw hat on. When the white people were near, he slowed his pace, made a small detour, lifted his hat as the white man and white woman passed. When they came close to Rudo, she slowed her pace, made a small detour and then continued walking. This happened many times before she got to Highlands. Not once did the white people answer or even look at her.

As she walked along, Rudo stole glances at the brightly painted bungalows hidden behind neatly trimmed hedges. She was afraid to look openly. There were bungalows on both sides of the road. At some of them, white people were sitting or lying on their lawns out in the sunshine. They were virtually naked! Only dressed at their private parts. The women had their breasts barely covered. At other houses, white people were swimming. She passed only a few houses that did not have cars in front of them. She saw a few black men and a few black women too. Some black men were cutting the lawns or trimming the hedges. Others were bringing drinks and food out on the lawns where the white people were. Others were watering gardens with hose-pipes. Most of the black women were playing with white children or hanging clothes on lines or pushing prams. Rudo wondered what kind of job she was going to get.

She came to the deep ravine, her uncle had told her she would come to before entering Highlands. She could see the tall gum trees he had also mentioned. Beyond the gum trees, she saw part of Highlands. The black man was still in front of her. But he had put more distance between them. She didn't need him now. She began to feel hungry and a little tired. The sightseeing had cost her much time. It was already afternoon. The thought of walking back all the way to Harare made her forget her immediate problem of hunger. She had to get a job that day, she told herself with determination.

She took a right turn off the main road beyond the gum trees and continued walking until she came to two rows of houses. The houses were bigger and even more attractive than those she had passed. The houses in Highlands stood in big yards with lawns, flowers and swimming pools at the front. At the back, there were orchards where many different fruit trees grew. Beyond the fruit trees, there were many *pikinini-kayas* (one-roomed shacks used to house domestic servants). Rudo followed the sanitary lane which ran at the back of the two rows of houses. She was going to ask if there was a job at every single house. She tried at the first house; a black nanny told her the Mrs there did not need anyone. At the second, there was no job, so the African cook said. At the third house, there was no one in. At the fourth house, the Mrs came out after being called by the garden-boy. She asked Rudo some questions but informed her that she didn't want her. At the fifth house, she asked a black woman who was hanging clothes on the line if there was a job.

'There might be soon. I have given Mrs my notice. If you want, you can wait for her.'

'I will wait, if it's all right.'

'Come on in the yard. Don't worry, they don't keep any dogs here . . . Do you want some water to drink?'

'Yes, please. Thank you.'

The woman went to fetch water from her employer's kitchen. The woman told Rudo to sit in the shade of the mango tree as it was very hot. She continued hanging the washing on the line.

The black woman was plump, round and very dark. She must have been in her late forties or early fifties. She was old enough to be Rudo's mother.

'Where do you come from, my child?'

'I am from Makosa's village.'

'Really? . . . I come from near there—at Chitekwe's village. Do you know it?'

'Very well. We have relatives there—uncles.'

'What is their name?'

'Hama.'

'Hama! My sister is married to Hama's son. Whose daughter are you?'

'My father is Gomo.'

'Gomo! Sekuru's son?'

'That is as it is.'

'By the spirits! You know I am your aunt! Let's talk about this later—have you eaten something?'

'Yes, I have. I am not hungry.'

'Don't be shy with me! My house is your house too. I haven't eaten yet either. Come, let's go inside the hut. You will cook us some *sadza* while I finish some small jobs.' The woman told Rudo that she was called Ma Saru.

Rudo spent the rest of that afternoon helping Ma Saru with small jobs. They talked all the time. By the time Mrs arrived, the two distant relatives had also become friends.

'Don't worry about the job. I will tell Mrs you are my sister—it makes it easier to explain. I will tell her that I can teach you how to do everything. I don't want you to worry about going back to Magaba today. You will stay here with me until you get a job. The one I have or another You hear me?'

Indeed, after Ma Saru had talked to Mrs van der Byl, Rudo was offered the job. While she was learning the 'responsible' household duties, Rudo was to be the washer-woman and nanny.

Ma Saru and Rudo shared the *pikinini-kaya*. It was a one-roomed corrugated iron shack which was originally a tool-shed. Like most 'PKs', it was situated at the edge of the yard, by the sanitary lane.

Rudo learned everything from Ma Saru. She learned to make the beds, tidy and clean the house exactly the way Mrs liked. She was taught how to dress the children properly. Rudo was shown the school where Master Peter and Master John went so that she could accompany them there in the mornings and fetch them after school. She was taught how to cook breakfast as well as various dishes for lunch and for supper. Rudo had to be shown the park and the playground where she would take the children in the afternoons and on Saturday mornings and during school holidays. She also learned where to go and how to do the regular household shopping.

There were only two rules Rudo had to observe. It was made very clear to her that she should never leave the yard without the permission of Mrs except in the course of her normal work duties. The second rule was that she should never entertain visitors, particularly male visitors, without informing Mrs first. It was only after Rudo had proved her competence at her work and her trustworthiness that Mrs finally agreed to discharge Ma Saru. Ma Saru warned Rudo never to leave a job without the complete consent of an employer. It didn't matter what notice you had given. Ma Saru knew a few women and men who had left at the end of their notice periods when their employers did not want them to leave. In every case, the employer had telephoned the police and said that this woman or that man had stolen some things from the house. Those people ended up in jail.

By the time Alexio arrived in Salisbury, Rudo was an expert in every aspect of her job. She could now speak English. Madam had been kind enough to allow Rudo to have Alexio live at the yard on condition he did not interfere with Rudo's work too much.

On the day Alexio was to arrive, Madam gave Rudo time to go and meet him. Rudo was allowed to use Madam's bicycle. When Rudo arrived with Alexio sitting on the bicycle carrier, the first thing she had to do was make him look presentable. She wiped his face and hair with a damp cloth and dressed him in one of her blouses, a white one, which Madam had given her. Leading the boy by the hand, she then took him to be 'seen' by Madam. They entered the house by the back door and waited for Madam in the kitchen. Soon, Madam walked in.

'This is the child, Madam,' reported Rudo in her usual soft-spoken voice.

'Oh! He is quite a man. Now Rudo, if you can't do your work because of him, he will have to go. Do you understand?'

'Yes, Madam.'

'How old is he?'

'I don't know, Madam.'

'What's his name?'

'Alexio, Madam.'

'Funny name—never mind. Do you think he might fit into some of Peter's or John's clothes? I should think he will. Let me go and see what I can dig up.'

Madam disappeared into Master Peter and Master John's rooms. When she came back, she gave Rudo three pairs of short trousers, two shirts and a sweater for Alexio. From somewhere Master Peter and Master John raced into the house and into the kitchen.

They saw Alexio.

'Hello!' 'Hello!'

'What's your name?'

'Have you come to live with Rudo?'

'Come, I will show you my room and my toys.'

'I am John.'

'I am Peter and—and I have more toys than John!'

It was hard to tell what Alexio was feeling or thinking. His mature face   remained expressionless. He looked unaffected and remained the same throughout.

'Can I feel your hair?' asked Master Peter and proceeded to put his hand on Alexio's head. Alexio forcefully warded off Master Peter's hand.

'That's enough, boys,' said Madam who had been watching the scene, 'come Peter, John. Back to your rooms! . . . I said out! Can't you see you are frightening the poor creature!'

The two white boys walked out of the kitchen. Alexio thought Madam was shouting at him. He clung to Rudo's legs.

'All right, Rudo. But please try not to bring him in the house too much. He causes the boys too much excitement.'

'Yes, Madam. Thank you, Madam.'

Rudo taught Alexio never to go to the house unless she called him. This proved to be very easy as Alexio was used to being by himself. He spent most of his time in front of the shack. He liked drawing all sorts of pictures on sand. At first he used to draw whole villages, people and animals. But in time, he began drawing things he saw around him—cars, bicycles and white people. When Rudo gave him a toy car, he used to spend hours building roads, moulding mountains out of sand and pretending to travel from one village to another. Sometimes Rudo used to take him along when she took Master Peter and Master John to the park or to the playground. But of course Rudo could not let him play with Master John, Master Peter and the other white children. It was not allowed. Alexio usually sat with Rudo and the other black nannies who also brought children to the park or to the playground.

Madam told her children not to play with Alexio as they frightened him. She also pointed out that Alexio couldn't speak English so the children wouldn't understand him anyway. Madam instructed Rudo never to allow the children to play with Alexio as there was a danger that a fight could occur. But Master Peter and Master John used to sneak out of the house and go to the shack to play with Alexio. Rudo knew about this but she used to turn a blind eye. She pretended to be angry when she had to 'discover' them and bring play to an end.

Gradually, the children got used to playing together. On the whole, they got on very well. Now and again, however, some minor fights broke out. Rudo always managed to stop the fights before anyone got hurt. These fights were easily mutually concealed from Madam. The children from neighbouring houses also used to secretly come and play. Play had to be centred outside the shack as Alexio refused to go anywhere else. Although language was a problem, the children somehow managed to communicate. As time passed, Alexio began to speak some English. Rudo was very pleased by this development. Life went on very much like this for about two years.

Then one day, Master Peter and Master John came from school and went to play with Alexio. They found Alexio asleep on the sand outside Rudo's shack. He did this quite often especially on hot afternoons. Master John and Master Peter had with them their latest toys—water pistols. They woke Alexio up by squirting water on his face. When Alexio woke up, he grabbed Master Peter and took his water pistol from him. He squirted water on Master Peter's face. Somehow, this annoyed Master Peter very much. Master Peter demanded his water pistol back. Alexio handed it over. Then Master John squirted water into Alexio's face. Again Alexio did what he had done with Master Peter. But when Master John demanded his pistol back, Alexio refused to hand it back. He said he didn't want to play that game. Master Peter supported his brother's demand for the pistol. Alexio still refused to hand it over. The two white boys attacked him. The fight was mainly between Alexio and Master Peter. After rolling over each other several times and scratching each other, Alexio gained advantage over Master Peter. He sat on Master Peter's tummy and went on hitting him on the face. Both children were screaming and covered in blood. Unfortunately, Rudo who usually stopped these fights, had gone out to the shops. Master John, after standing about helplessly for some minutes, tried to pull Alexio off Master Peter. He had asked for it. Alexio went for Master John and soon had him on the floor. But Master Peter stood up and saw a heavy plank just outside Rudo's shack. With it, he began pounding Alexio. Alexio went for the plank. It was while the struggle for the plank was going on that the Mrs from next door who had heard the screams arrived and stopped the fight. For some reason her immediate instinct was to slap Alexio several times. Just then, Rudo arrived. Again, like the Mrs, Rudo's immediate reaction was to beat Alexio. Frantically, she hit the boy until he couldn't cry any more.

She and the Mrs took Master Peter and Master John inside the house. They cleaned up the children and treated their scratches. There was no question of hiding this fight from Madam, Rudo knew. Was she going to lose her job? When Madam came home, she was shocked by the state of her children. Shivering with fear, Rudo reported the little she knew about the fight to Madam.

'I could send you to jail for this, you know! I have always known there was something sinister about that little bastard! Get the bicycle and take him away from here! Don't let me ever see him again! Come on! Out!'

Rudo went out. Madam telephoned the doctor. Alexio was still lying where he had fallen after Rudo beat him. He wasn't crying. He lay very still. Rudo walked past him and disappeared inside the shack. When she came out, she had a cloth bag in which she had thrown the few things that belonged to Alexio.

As she walked towards where he lay, she gently called out his name. He did not stir. All of a sudden Rudo became very scared. Had she hit him *that* hard? He wasn't . . . No! What had she done? She picked him up and felt a great relief. He looked her straight in the eye but she looked away. She went to Madam's garage where the bicycle was kept and placed him in the carrier. She tied his feet with a rag so that they would not get into the spokes by accident. She pushed the bicycle out of the yard and rode to Magaba.

Her plan was to leave him at Magaba. She would ask Shiri if his daughter, Rewayi, could take Alexio to Chipo at Macheke. Chipo, Rudo's younger sister, was married to a man named Munda. Munda and Chipo lived on a white man's farm—Boss Newton's farm, outside Macheke. Munda worked as the farm shopkeeper. The shop belonged to Boss Newton. Munda and Chipo would have to help, Rudo decided. For a few months anyway. She knew there was no point in sending Alexio to Makosa.

When she arrived at Shiri's house, she explained the problem.

'Do you have a little money?' asked Shiri when Rudo finished explaining.

'Enough to pay for Alexio and Rewayi to catch a bus to Macheke. I am sure Chipo and Munda will give Rewayi money to return here.'

'Why, there is no problem then. When do you want them to depart?'

'Tomorrow?'

'Well, let it be tomorrow . . . Rewayi?'

'Yes, father?'

'You leave for Macheke tomorrow. You are taking Alexio to Chipo. Be ready to leave early in the morning. You hear?'

'Yes, father.'

It was late when Rudo arrived back in Highlands. She had been delayed by the police on the way. The police had every right to stop any African at that time of the night—especially around white residential areas. They stopped Rudo and demanded to see her 'town pass'. She produced it. It was illegal for her to go anywhere without it. They questioned her and took down all her particulars. It was only after they had telephoned Madam to ask her to confirm all the details about Rudo, that they let her go.

As soon as she arrived, Rudo went into her shack and lay down. She was so tired and so confused and very worried. She started crying as she thought about Alexio. She felt remorseful. She already missed him. She had lived with him for over two years. He called her 'Mother'. She had cuddled him night after night. Rudo loved the boy; she now felt empty without him. She cried and cried until she fell fast asleep.

The next morning, Shiri accompanied Rewayi and Alexio to the bus station at Harare Market. He told Rewayi to ask for Boss Newton's farm when she and the child got off the bus in Macheke. They arrived there soon after midday. She learned that Boss Newton's farm was some six miles out of Macheke. The only way to get there was to walk. Carrying Alexio who was still in pain from his beating, on her back and a small bundle of their clothes on her head, Rewayi started walking to Boss Newton's farm. She walked slowly and arrived at the farm late in the afternoon. She found her way to the farm shop. Inside the shop, she introduced herself and Alexio to Munda. He was very pleased to see them. After exchanging greetings he took them to the back of the store where his huts were. Chipo, who was very pregnant, was pleasantly surprised by their arrival. She attended to Alexio's pains. His face was still swollen and bruised. After that she prepared some food for them.

Munda and Chipo spent the evening exchanging news with Rewayi. Chipo insisted that Rewayi should stay a few days. Munda suggested that Rewayi should leave on a Friday morning because the farm truck went into Macheke then. He was good friends with the driver and she would get a lift with him. Rewayi agreed. The following Friday, the girl was given her fare and some extra money, got a lift with the truck-driver and returned to Salisbury.

Boss Newton's farm was very big. He grew tobacco and maize, but mainly tobacco. He also reared dairy cattle, sheep and chickens. He employed many people.

Every day, except Sundays, the head foreman used to sound

reveille two hours, or maybe three hours before sunrise. All
the farm workers were supposed to be at the fields within half
an hour of reveille being sounded. There was a foreman at
each field. The first thing he did after the workers had arrived
at the fields was to make roll-call. Then he gave everyone
present their piece-work. When a worker finished his piece,
he reported to the foreman who inspected the piece before
dismissing the worker. The fastest workers usually finished
their work at about lunchtime. Then they would be free.
There was never much to do with the free time. Some people
went fishing down the river which cut through the farm;
others gambled at cards afternoon after afternoon. Those who
had relatives on surrounding farms visited or received them.

On Friday afternoons, everyone received their rations of
maize meal, beans and salt. People queued at the grinding
mill near Boss Newton's house to receive the rations which
were supposed to be enough for a week but were never
adequate. The size of a ration depended on how large a family
was. Once a week, usually at weekends, one or two people
were given permission to brew and sell beer. But if there was
any disorder, no matter how minor, whosoever had brewed
the beer was fined by Boss Newton. At weekends, people had
nothing better to do than spend their hard-earned wages on
beer.

The really big day was the Friday before the end of each
month. That was the day everyone got paid. Boss Newton
made sure everybody had a chance to buy what they wanted to
by ordering Munda to keep the store open until the last
customer was out. On days like that, Chipo had to work with
Munda. There were just too many people. If they bought their
clothes, utensils and other things for cash, Munda wouldn't
have needed any help. But they didn't. Their wages were not
enough to buy what they wanted. So they were given credits.
Some people were there to pay bicycle credits which were four
years old, others were there to pay off one credit and start
another. Those who were relatively new had their debits
deducted from their wages and so they just came to the store
to see who was buying what. It was the paper-work that Chipo
helped with.

There were never enough workers on the farm. Most of the workers were bachelors who came and went. Boss Newton encouraged people to bring their families and settle on the farm. Some men had to keep their wives at 'Reserves' because they wanted their children to attend school. Boss Newton solved this problem by opening a school on the farm. As it turned out the farm school was only good enough to produce more farm labourers. All the same Ma Munda, who was already sending her three children to the school, suggested it would not harm Alexio to attend this school. So Chipo and Munda sent him to the farm school.

Ma Munda was a deeply religious woman. She was an ardent Anglican. Every Sunday she walked the twelve miles to and from Macheke for services. She never missed church unless the river was flooded and she couldn't cross it. Ma Munda, a very large, ever-laughing woman, was, like her husband, in her late fifties.

There was a certain time that Munda, Chipo and their son went on leave. Ma Munda's daughter and two younger sons happened to have gone to visit their grandmother at the village where their mother came from. Alexio was left in the care of Munda's parents.

On a Sunday, Ma Munda woke up early and prepared to go to church. She decided to take Alexio along with her. She and the child started for church. But about half way there, Ma Munda felt very ill and decided to go back home. When they arrived back home, she wished she had not come back. She found her husband sleeping with another woman in their hut. A very heated quarrel took place inside the hut. Ma Munda had ordered Alexio to go to the compound and play with his friends when the arguments started. But the boy had only pretended to leave. He remained outside the hut. After a time he heard the groans of a woman in pain.

He tip-toed back to the door of the hut in which the groaning came from. He knelt at the closed door. Through a small crack in the door, he peered inside. What he saw horrified him. Ma Munda had a rope around her neck. Chimwe and the woman he had been found with were trying hard to pull the rope over a beam in the roof of the hut. But

Ma Munda was too heavy for them. Alexio's reaction was immediate and involuntary. He screamed at the top of his voice! The door swung open and Chimwe tried to grab Alexio. The boy tried to run away but after a short chase Chimwe caught him.

'Don't scream! I have some sweets for you! Let's go inside the hut! I will give you some sweets,' Chimwe kept on repeating in a very strange voice.

When they were inside the hut, Chimwe tied a piece of cloth over Alexio's mouth. He asked his woman to hold Alexio firmly. She did so. Chimwe went out and came back with a short heavy lead pipe. With it, he started bashing Ma Munda on the head! His woman did not want to look, so she covered her eyes so that she wouldn't see what was happening. Alexio was free. The little boy bolted out of the hut. He ran towards the compound, but Chimwe was hot behind him. Alexio realized he would not get very far before he was caught. He saw a sizable stone by the side of the track which ran from the compound to Boss Newton's house. He sat down near the stone. Chimwe arrived and was just about to pick him up when Alexio, with all his little might, pounded Chimwe on the foot with the stone. The pain was enough for Chimwe to let go Alexio. The boy continued running towards the compound before turning off into the long grass on the sides of the track. There he hid, not knowing what else to do.

At the compound there was a woman with whom Ma Munda sometimes went to church. Alexio decided to go to her huts. But when he was near her huts, he saw Chimwe coming out of her hut and ride his bicycle back to his huts. Alexio dashed behind a nearby hut until Chimwe had passed. Then he went to the woman's hut.

As soon as he appeared in the doorway of her hut, the woman began chiding Alexio. She said Ma Munda and Chimwe were very worried about him. Alexio was a silly boy! The woman was going to take Alexio back home right away. Alexio tried to speak but the woman wouldn't listen nor would she stop chiding him. She gripped his arm and began leading him back home. The boy screamed and struggled, but her grip was very strong. Alexio gave up the fight. He was crying.

When they were near Chimwe's huts, Alexio decided to bite the woman's hand. He bit her savagely! She screamed and let go his arm. The boy sprinted away towards the river. She didn't bother to chase him. She decided that she might as well tell Ma Munda and Chimwe what had happened.

When Chimwe heard the sound of her foot-steps, he rushed out of the hut. He looked very strange—agitated and nervous. He more or less demanded to know what she wanted. This was in sharp contrast to his behaviour when he had gone to her house. She told him about Alexio. He became very excited and asked which way the boy had run. She told him: towards the river. Chimwe began running towards the river, but changed his mind. The woman asked if she could talk to Ma Munda. Chimwe told her Ma Munda had gone to look for Alexio. The woman left. But the look on Chimwe's face had frightened her very much. She thought about the situation as she walked back to the compound.

Chimwe was creeping behind her at a distance. When the woman was some way from his huts, he ran down towards the river. The woman met a man, who was one of the foremen, on the track. She pleaded with him to go after Alexio and Chimwe. But the man refused. She told the foreman that she thought Alexio may be in some danger. The foreman then reluctantly agreed to go.

Alexio was hiding in the dense reeds on the river bank. He could hear Chimwe calling:

'Alexio! Alexio! Alexio!'

He kept on calling but the boy did not answer. Alexio could tell that Chimwe was not very far away.

Chimwe decided to trick the boy:

'Alex-io!' called out a woman's voice.

This was how Ma Munda usually called Alexio.

'Alex-io! Can you hear me?' shouted the woman's voice again.

'Alexio! Answer if you can hear me!' The boy listened. The voices were now very near.

'He is a very silly boy. Alexio! What does he think you did to me?' said the female voice.

'He thinks I might have harmed you! Children are like

that!' responded the male voice that Alexio recognized as Chimwe's.

'Alex-io! Can you hear me?' It was the female voice again.

'Yes!' he replied.

'Where are you?' asked Chimwe.

'Here in the reeds!'

'Come on! Let's go home. Your meal is getting cold!' said the woman's voice.

Alexio was rushing and ploughing through the reeds. The reeds were very tall and he couldn't see where he was going. Suddenly, Alexio felt an arm around his waist and a hand over his mouth. It was Chimwe. Alone.

'You need a wash. You need a wash,' Chimwe kept repeating. His eyes were rolling in a very strange way.

Chimwe took the boy into the river. He found a place where the river was deep. He placed Alexio on the ground and squatted on the boy's back. Chimwe dipped Alexio's head into the water. He had his hands on Alexio's neck. Now and again Chimwe brought Alexio's head out of the water and looked at the boy's face. He also looked out all around for any people.

From only a few feet away, the foreman who couldn't see Alexio under Chimwe, asked:

'You haven't found—'

Chimwe jumped up. Alexio fell into the river. Chimwe hurriedly limped away. The foreman rescued Alexio from the water. The foreman pressed Alexio's stomach several times but the boy didn't vomit. The foreman stuck his forefingers down Alexio's throat, then the child began vomiting. While this was going on, Chimwe took the foreman's bicycle and rode off to Boss Newton's house. He reported to Boss Newton that he, Chimwe, had found the foreman drowning Alexio and that the boy was already dead. Boss Newton immediately telephoned the Macheke police.

When Alexio came round and looked a little better, the foreman carried him to where he had left his bicycle and discovered that it was not there. Carrying the child in his arms, he walked to the compound. He took Alexio to the hut of Ma Munda's friend. A short time after he arrived there, the police arrived. They immediately handcuffed him and put him in the police landrover. All his protests were answered by beatings. Ma Munda's friend tried to explain too, but the police did not want to listen to her. Chimwe had come with the police. He asked the woman to hand Alexio over to him. But the woman refused. She said she would only give Alexio to Ma Munda. When Chimwe tried to force the matter, the police told him to leave the child with the woman as his wife was not at home and he had to go into Macheke with the police to make a witness's statement on what he had seen the foreman do.

When Chimwe returned from Macheke, he went to demand Alexio back. But the woman and her husband, having listened to what Alexio had told them, refused to hand him over. The husband and wife knew that Munda and Chipo were returning the next day. They did not sleep that night, but kept guard on Alexio.

When Munda and Chipo returned; Chimwe told them his version of what had happened.

But when Chipo went to collect Alexio, she heard a very different story. Fearing for the boy's life, she decided that she wasn't going to take him home. She hid him at one of her own friends' huts in the compound. Chipo also made up her mind that Alexio was to leave the farm as soon as possible. The only place she could send the boy was to Makosa's village.

When Chipo got to her huts, her husband wondered why she had not brought Alexio. She tried to avoid telling him the reasons, but he pressed her. She told him what she had heard. Munda was outraged. He gave her a thorough beating for believing that his father could have tried to kill Alexio. That night husband and wife slept in separate huts. Munda slept in the hut where Alexio normally slept. In the middle of the night he heard someone open the door and enter the hut. In a very low voice, the dark figure was calling Alexio's name. Munda discovered that it was his father. He asked his father what he was doing there at such a time of the night. Chimwe said he wanted to ask the boy if he had seen the foreman do something to Ma Munda. Munda began to think that there might be something in what his wife had heard. Fearing that Chimwe might believe Alexio was in the hut where Chipo and their son were asleep. He decided to join them as soon as his father had left. A short time after transferring into his wife's hut, the door of that hut began to open again. Munda tried to warn off his father by talking to his wife. But Chimwe thought his daughter-in-law was sleeping with another man and started attacking Munda. Questioned again, Chimwe explained his presence there by saying that he had been watching a man whom he thought was having an affair with Chipo. That was not the end. Chimwe went to Ma Munda's friend's house. But again, Alexio was not there.

A number of days passed. Chimwe went to his in-laws' village to look for his wife. But they said she had never arrived there. He came back to the farm. He said all he could do was wait for her to return.

Nearly two weeks later, a shepherd-boy of fifteen years old, was herding sheep not too far from Boss Newton's house, which was also near Chimwe's house. He thought he smelt a terrible stench but didn't think much about it. The next thing that happened was that he heard some dogs barking. He rushed over to where they were because he thought they had cornered a hare. As he got closer, the stench became stronger and he realized the dogs were not just barking but fighting. Then he saw what they were fighting over. A corpse! All the flesh of the face had been eaten by the dogs. The rest of the body was still buried in a shallow grave.

The shepherd ran to Boss Newton's house, and reported what he had seen. The police were called out again. Chimwe was taken for questioning. The police were just about to let him go back to the farm and charge the foreman with murder, when Chimwe's mistress walked into the police station and confessed everything that had actually happened. She and Chimwe were charged with murdering his wife. Chimwe was also charged with the attempted murder of Alexio. The foreman was released.

The police decided that six-year-old Alexio was too young to give evidence at Chimwe's trial. A few days after this decision Chipo sent Alexio to Makosa.

The three years that Alexio had spent away from Makosa's village had given him certain experiences that made him a

very different boy from the other children in the village. For
Alexio, life in the village was relatively simple compared to
life in Salisbury and at Boss Newton's farm. Somehow this
made him a very self-possessed little boy. Even when he was
with children of his own age, his knowledge of various
subjects made him seem more intelligent and more mature
than the other children. Like most children, he was obedient,
courteous and respectful to his elders. His manners and
behaviour endeared him to many people in the village. But
this and his clothes, aroused much jealousy and envy from
Gomo and the rest of his family. Rudo and Chipo, who both
felt they were responsible for Alexio's up-bringing did not help
matters very much. They sent some money to Gomo for Alexio
to begin school at Makosa. This generosity of his daughters
towards their cousin did not please Gomo. Some of the girl's
own brothers and sisters, step-brothers and step-sisters were
not going to school because of lack of money. Ma Rudo too.
She complained bitterly about how sending Alexio to school
was a waste of money. A few weeks after Alexio had arrived at
Makosa, Gomo thought out a convenient solution to the
problem.

A man named Murimi was a friend of Gomo. Murimi and
his wife had not been able to have children. As these were now
modern times, they had not bothered to visit any medicine-
men nor had Murimi contemplated taking a second wife.
Murimi and his wife, Ruwa, lived in a village some seven miles
from Makosa—at Jena's village. Gomo visited his friend to
make a suggestion: if Murimi wished, he could foster Alexio
on condition that Murimi sent the boy to school and kept him
clothed. Murimi and his wife gladly took up this offer. Within
a few days, Alexio was moved from Makosa's to Jena's village.

Murimi had the reputation of being one of the hardest
workers in Jena's village. On the December evening Alexio
arrived at Murimi's huts, he was accompanied by Gomo. As
soon as the evening meal was over, Murimi advised Alexio to
go to sleep. Alexio thought perhaps Murimi and Gomo had
something to discuss and did not want him at the 'dare'.
Alexio went to his hut and lay down. He wondered what life
was going to be like with Murimi and Ruwa. Eventually he

fell asleep. Some time, long before the first crow of the cock, Murimi came and woke Alexio up. Alexio wondered why he was being woken up so soon after going to sleep.

'It's the beginning of the day, my friend. Get up!' said Murimi.

Alexio grumbled sleepily.

'Come on! We have no time to waste!' ordered Murimi.

Alexio got up and started looking for his clothes in the unlit hut.

'From now onwards, you will sleep in your clothes! Is that understood?'

'Yes, uncle.'

'You can put your shirt on as we walk to the pen! Hurry up!'

Murimi led Alexio to the cattle pen a hundred yards or so from the huts. Murimi removed the poles that closed the entrance to the cattle pen and told Alexio to get in and drive out two oxen which Murimi pointed out. Alexio did not want his feet to sink into the rain-soaked dung. Therefore, he tried, lamely, to drive the oxen from the edges of the cattle pen where the dung was not so deep. Murimi followed Alexio into the cattle pen and pushed him to where the dung was deep.

'You are not in Salisbury or at the farm anymore. Here people work! If you want to keep your feet clean you have come to the wrong place. Come on! Drive those oxen!'

Feeling very hurt, Alexio finally drove the oxen out. Murimi kept a yoke by the pen. He had brought with him from the huts two straps and a whip. He yoked the oxen.

'Drive the oxen along that path. I shall catch up with you soon,' said Murimi as he walked back to the huts. Alexio was afraid of the dark but did not dare say so. He drove the oxen along the track until Murimi caught up with him.

'The whole point about driving oxen, Alexio, is to make them move faster than they want to!' said Murimi as he snatched the whip from Alexio and set the oxen into a trot. At the field, they ploughed for a good three hours before anyone else appeared. At about sunrise, both Alexio and the oxen were very tired.

'Give me the whip!' shouted Murimi.

Alexio thought Murimi was going to give him a short rest. He handed the whip over. Murimi gave the boy a couple of lashes around the legs.

'That should wake you up a bit!' he said and threw the whip back at Alexio.

Finally the oxen could barely walk, Murimi decided to give them a short rest. There was a hilly patch of land which was unsuitable for cultivation by Murimi's field. He ordered Alexio to take the oxen there and let them graze. Meanwhile, using a long graduated wire to guide them, Murimi and Alexio started sowing groundnuts on the patch they had just ploughed. After an hour, Murimi ordered Alexio to fetch the oxen. They resumed ploughing until three hours after sunrise. By that time, everyone on the surrounding fields had unyoked their oxen at least an hour before.

Laden with a large basket containing everything she would need to prepare the midday meal and some water, as well as driving the rest of the herd of cattle, Ruwa arrived at the field. She left the animals grazing on the hilly patch and joined Murimi and Alexio in sowing. Alexio had to also keep an eye on the cattle and to make sure they did not wander off to other people's fields. At about midday, Ruwa started preparing the midday meal; Alexio took the cattle to the stream which was towards the village to let them have a drink; and Murimi went on sowing. By the time Alexio arrived back at the field, the midday meal was ready. After lunch Murimi and Ruwa took a short rest. Alexio too, when the cattle were not wandering off too far.

Soon, they started sowing again. When the afternoon became a little cooler, Murimi and Alexio yoked a different pair of oxen and started ploughing again. Shortly before sunset, they unyoked the oxen and Alexio was told to take the cattle to graze near Murimi's huts. He was also told to begin watering the vegetables in the garden surrounding the huts as soon as he got home. Murimi's vegetable garden was by far the largest in the village. With a bucket, Alexio fetched water from the well which was in the centre of the garden and watered the vegetables. When he finished that, he took the cattle to the pen. The young man had been told to bring logs

for the fire at the *dare* on his way from the pen every evening.
He was to light the fire at the *dare* as well. Alexio picked up a
few logs and lit the fire. As soon as Murimi arrived at the *dare*,
the evening meal was served. After supper, Alexio, now
exhausted, bade Murimi and Ruwa goodnight.

'You can't go to sleep yet, my friend. I told you we are not
soft here. We are going to crack some nuts and select seeds for
tomorrow's sowing.'

Ruwa was grinding maize for the next day's meals. Murimi
and Alexio sat at the *dare* cracking nuts. They did not stop
until they had finished the amount that Murimi had set as the
target for that evening. After that, Alexio went to sleep. But
Murimi and his wife stayed up. The next day was much the
same. In fact, life went on like that until Alexio started going
to school.

The nearest school was the mission school at Makosa. So
Alexio and other children from the village had to walk there
every morning and back every afternoon.

On the first day Alexio was to go to school, he and his
uncle, Murimi, got up at the usual time. They went to the
field and finished ploughing. The whole field was now
completely ploughed. Another few days and all the sowing
would be done as well. No one else in the village was anywhere
near to finishing these jobs. Murimi and Alexio returned
home after stopping at the freshwater stream to wash. The
previous evening, Murimi and Alexio had picked and packed
tomatoes and cabbages which were to be taken to the bus stop
at Makosa and then sent to Salisbury. In Salisbury, Murimi
had an arrangement with another man to sell the vegetables at
the market. So Murimi and Alexio loaded the vegetable boxes
onto a sledge and drove a pair of oxen to Makosa. Alexio left
Murimi at the bus-stop and went to school. School ended
some time after midday. Alexio walked back to Jena's village
with the other children after school. Murimi chided him for
being late. From that day onwards, Alexio was to be the first
child to arrive in the village from school. And unless told otherwise, he was to go straight from school to the field. Alexio
told Murimi that Wednesday was the sports day at school
and all the children were required to stay there in the afternoon.

'Tell the teacher or whosoever is responsible that I say no! What else did they say about wasting time at school?'

'Unless we go to church every Sunday, we shall be punished,' responded Alexio.

'Sunday is the only day we have to thoroughly weed the vegetable garden. They will have to punish you.'

After the first day of school, Alexio spent the rest of it sowing with Murimi and Ruwa. By the end of the first school week, Alexio found himself in a trap. On Thursday afternoon and the following Monday afternoon, he had to stay at school to do his punishment for missing sports and church respectively. On each afternoon, Murimi beat him up for not coming home early. This led to Alexio running away and going back to Gomo. Gomo and Murimi discussed the problem and Alexio was allowed to attend both sports and church.

These were his favourite days. The cattle were no problem at all. Usually they stuck together and wandered very little. Alexio always took his books to read and catch up on his homework, this was the only time that he had to do his homework. These were the days when he used to dream about his future. Although he hated being over-worked, he realized that he was gaining a capacity for work which would prove useful in the future. And anyway, he had no choice. Gomo had clearly told him that if he left Murimi, that was the end of his schooling. What kind of life would he have if he left school? The key to the future was to keep at school and do well. The mission school only went up to standard three. That meant he had to remain at Murimi's for the next five years! In some ways it was a long time, but compared to what he was going to gain from his schooling, it was a short time. He used to multiply the years by the months in a year, and then work out how many days there were in five years. Would he ever see his mother? He would try to visualize what she looked like. Did she ever think about him? He would wonder what she was doing at that very moment. And to think there was a straight line between where she was and where he was!

One day during school holidays, Murimi, Ruwa and Alexio were weeding the field. Murimi always liked to set targets when doing any work. On that day he decided on piece work. Murimi gave Alexio a smaller piece than his and Ruwa's. Alexio pointed out how small it was. Murimi doubled it and challenged the boy to finish the piece before the end of the day. And if he did, Murimi would give Alexio anything he asked for.

'Do you really mean that, uncle?'

'Yes. I mean that.'

'Can you let me go and visit my mother?'

Murimi knew all Alexio's circumstances but he had never thought about Tendayi, the boy's mother. After a short time Murimi replied:

'Yes. If you finish it properly, I will let you go and spend a week with your mother.'

'When?'

'There is no point in discussing the details until you have succeeded in finishing your piece properly.'

The strength Alexio felt because of the possibility of being allowed to go and visit his mother was amazing. Thorough and a perfectionist by nature, Alexio finished his piece long before the end of the day. After making a very careful inspection, Murimi said:

'Yes, you have done your work well. Since you have finished your work for the day, I want you to go to Makosa and ask for Gomo's permission. If he approves I will let you go to see your mother. If he doesn't we will just say you have asked for something I can't give.'

Alexio knew Gomo would not give his approval. But all the same, walking to and from Makosa would give him time to himself, which he liked. So he went to Makosa. After Alexio had asked for Gomo's permission, the reply he got was:

'Who put that idea into your head?!'

'No one, father.'

'Was it Murimi?'

'No. It was not uncle Murimi.'

'Now listen to me, child. This is the first and last time I shall hear you ask to see your mother again! Do you hear me?'

'Yes, father.'

Alexio started crying. Gomo got hold of the boy and hit him several times.

'You are not a woman! The only time a man cries is when he is mourning! Now wipe away those stupid tears!'

Alexio did as he was told. He felt very upset as he walked back to Jena's village. On the way, a car passed him. He remembered it was Thursday. That was when Dr Smith came to the clinic. On Thursdays. That put an idea into his head. Yes, he could run away. Dr Smith came from and returned to Mtoko every Thursday. He thought about the idea as he walked back to Murimi's.

From how unhappy Alexio looked, Murimi knew Gomo had refused to allow the boy to go and see his mother.

'Look, Alexio. Since you can't go and see your mother, I have a suggestion. I will let you use the oxen and the plough to earn yourself some money. All you need is to find another boy to help you. You can give him a third of what you get paid. You know some people are still ploughing and will welcome help. I will fix all the arrangements for you. Ploughing for three days, you could earn yourself enough money to buy a shirt and a pair of short trousers.'

Alexio accepted. But his mind was on running away. He made up his mind that he would stay with his mother for exactly one week and no more.

The following Thursday, Alexio disappeared very early in the morning. He avoided going through Makosa by following a small path that cut through the woods. This path led him to the track which ran through Makosa to Mtoko. Soon, he came to the track and he started walking towards Mtoko. After some distance, he decided to sit down and wait for Dr Smith. But after thinking about it, it occurred to him that Dr Smith might not even stop for him or his car would be full-up. So he decided to walk on. He saw Dr Smith's car coming from Mtoko heading for Makosa. He waved him down. The doctor stopped.

'What's a little boy like you doing in the middle of nowhere? Aren't you afraid?'

'No, Dr Smith. I want to go to see my mother. Can you promise me a lift on your way back?'

'Look, come with me to Makosa and we will drive back together.'

'No, Dr Smith. I will walk towards Mtoko. But please, stop for me on your way back.'

'As you please, sir! I won't forget to stop for you. But you must remain on the road. Understood?'

'Yes, Dr Smith. Thank you.'

Alexio felt very happy. He was going to see his mother that day! She didn't even know he was coming!

He didn't have to hurry now. He decided the best thing was to pick up his lunch of wild fruit before Dr Smith was on his way back. If he left it till later, he might not be by the roadside when Dr Smith came past.

Later that afternoon, Dr Smith picked up Alexio and dropped him off at Mtoko. Alexio had learned that visitors usually arrived at a place in the evening. He decided to wait for dusk. He spent the rest of the day picking wild fruit for his mother. At sunset he walked towards where he thought his mother lived. He asked a man at the nearest house he came to:

'Can you tell me where my mother lives?'

The man laughed and asked:

'Who is your mother?'

'Oh! . . . er. I don't really know her name.'

'Where are you coming from?' asked the man.

'From Makosa's village, sire,' replied Alexio in the manner of a grown-up man.

'You must be Tendayi's little boy, then. Is your name Chiko?'

'It used to be. I am now called Alexio.'

'Your mother will die with joy when she sees you. Does she know you are arriving today?'

'No. I don't think so.'

'Well, if you will let me, I will walk with you.'

The man walked with Alexio. As they got deeper into the village, their pace was slowed by many people greeting the little stranger. In the end, word got ahead to his mother that Chiko had arrived in the village. People rushed to greet him. Finally, he came to his mother's hut. He entered and left everyone outside.

The little man sat down with some dignity. Ma Chiko took a gourd of water, knelt before him and offered him some water to drink. After taking a sip, he handed the gourd back to her.

Mother and son then greeted each other quite unemotionally. With total trust, Alexio told his mother the long story of his life as she prepared some food for him. When he had finished, she broke down and cried.

In the next three days, Alexio learned much about his father, about his mother, about his relatives and about himself. For those three days, Alexio and his mother were inseparable.

'Whatever happens, you are the head of the family.' She kept on telling him time after time and treated him as if he really was the head of some big family.

'I hope I shall live to see the day you will take a wife. I want you to have many children . . . All this suffering will pass—I know we may not see each other for many years. It is very painful to think that. But, as I said, I am only your mother; you have to work now for your life ahead.'

On the evening of the fourth day, Gomo arrived at Tendayi's hut. Tendayi had hoped things wouldn't turn out this way. Alexio left his mother to explain to Gomo that he had intended to go back to Murimi after seven days and that he had had no intention of staying with his mother for good. Gomo was very friendly and accepted this. He even offered Tendayi permission to visit Alexio at Jena's village once every six months. Tendayi pleaded with Gomo not to be harsh with Alexio for having run away. Gomo promised that he would not punish the boy unless he ran away again.

Early the next morning, Gomo and Alexio left Mtoko for Makosa. Gomo asked Alexio to explain how he had run away. Alexio did. They talked about many things on their way to Makosa. At Makosa, Alexio said he should leave for Jena's straight away. But Gomo told him to leave the next day. After the evening meal that day, Gomo summoned Alexio into his hut and ordered the boy to remove his clothes. As if possessed by a demon, Gomo started beating Alexio with a thick stick. After a while, Ma Rudo came to plead with Gomo to stop beating the child but Gomo stopped only to tell her to go away. Finally, when Gomo came out of the hut, his clothes and sweat-covered face were spurted with blood. Ma Rudo went in to the hut and took Alexio. She washed and comforted him. Alexio couldn't sleep because of his wounds. When everyone was ready to go to sleep, Alexio decided to go to Jena's. Everyone thought he was trying to go back to Mtoko. Gomo followed and asked Alexio where he thought he was going. But Alexio did not answer him. Gomo was just about to threaten a further beating when he realized that Alexio was on the path to Jena's village. He followed the boy for some distance until he was satisfied that Alexio was going to Murimi's huts.

When Alexio arrived at Murimi's huts, it was late and very dark. Murimi and his wife had gone to sleep. But Alexio wanted them to know that he was back. When he knocked on the door of their hut, Murimi came out. All Murimi and Alexio could see of each other in the dark were their silhouettes.

'Uncle Murimi, I have come back,' said Alexio.

'Do you know how much inconvenience your sudden departure has caused me? Do you know?'

'I am sorry, uncle.'

'Sorry?! What good is that going to do me?!'

Murimi, who did not know that Alexio had already been beaten by Gomo, started hitting the boy. Murimi did not hit Alexio for very long before his wounds started bleeding again. Murimi stopped because his hands were wet with blood. He was very surprised.

'Are you bleeding?'

'Yes, uncle.'

'Well, I hardly hit you that hard.'

'No. It's from the earlier beating.'

'From Gomo?'

'Yes, uncle.'

'Look, I am sorry I hit you. I didn't think you would go to Gomo's first if you ever came back. But you know Alexio, you deserve it. You should never do things without permission.'

Alexio started crying and walked to his hut. He couldn't lie down, he couldn't sit, so he squatted and stood all night. At the usual time, Murimi came to wake him up and they went to the fields. When the sun rose, Murimi saw how badly Alexio had been beaten.

'Alexio! Why didn't you tell me?'

'Tell you what, uncle,' said the boy, very surprised.

'You must be in terrible pain!'

Alexio felt like bursting into tears again and didn't say anything.

'Go back home this minute and go to the clinic. Don't come back to the field. Tell your aunt to leave you food at the huts.'

On the way to the huts and on the way to the clinic, Alexio met many people. They all felt sorry for him and said sympathetic words to him. He hated it. It made him feel like crying. Rumours began to spread that Murimi had nearly killed Alexio. Some people even asked him about it. Murimi was eventually obliged to go through the village and explain that it was Gomo who had beaten the boy.

In time, Alexio's wounds healed. The villagers' sympathy turned into admiration for his courage in the face of much ill-treatment. Sometimes on his way from school, Alexio was waylaid by women who insisted on giving him food because they believed he was not being well fed. Alexio's domestic life remained much the same for the next five years.

Alexio never felt that they spent enough time at school. He also thought that they could spend more time learning than doing some of the things they had to. Every day school started with assembly in front of the new school block. When Rev Cope first opened the Mission at Makosa, he had got a small mud-and-thatch church, designed like a cross, built. Several years later when he decided to open the school, the classes were held in the four wings of the cross-like church. He had to face many problems. To start with, he was the only teacher. At first, the villagers at Makosa were not eager to send their children to school. So it had not been too difficult for Rev Cope to manage on his own. But later more and more people began sending their children to school. Not only did Rev Cope have too many children and no help, but the number of classes had also multiplied. He had travelled to Salisbury to seek money in order to build a proper school, buy books, blackboards, chalk and other materials. He had also tried to find some teachers. He had come back empty-handed and disappointed except for two young African men he had met at Mtoko. He made up his mind that he would train the two young men to teach. He had to pay them but didn't have the money. It was in that year that he decided to introduce school fees. But the parents of the children did not have the money. Rev Cope suggested they had to sell some of their grain or groundnuts at Boss Kaplan's store. And they had had to. Rev Cope had also decided to build a proper school with free labour from the village. All those who helped to build the school block did not have to pay any fees. But those who did not had to pay. The new block could not be built entirely without money—especially as Rev Cope was trying to make it into a proper school building. He had devised methods of raising money but his plans had not all worked out at first. It had taken many years to complete the building—a three-roomed brick block. After the completion of the building, help for materials and teachers had been easier to get. At the time when Alexio first went there, the school had been in existence for about ten years. It ran classes from grade one to grade five.

At assembly, the children stood in straight lines according to classes. The head teacher, one of the Africans Rev Cope had recruited from Mtoko, conducted an inspection to see if each child was clean and properly dressed. The children had to be dressed in school uniform: khaki shorts and khaki shirts for the boys and plain deep blue dresses for the girls. They had to comb their hair and be generally clean. If a pupil did not meet these standards, the head teacher used to send them back home. There were quite a few cases every year where parents had enough money to pay the school fees but not enough to buy the uniform. Their children had not been accepted at the school.

After inspection, there was roll call. Roll call was followed by announcements which always started with naming those who had to stay at school to do punishment for having been absent the previous day or breaking any of the numerous school rules. After this, the whole school made an orderly march into the church for service. The children sang a hymn; the bible was read and explained; the children were led into another hymn, then a prayer before physical training in the school playground. It was after all this that classes began.

Alexio's academic life at Makosa showed a very steady improvement throughout his five years of schooling. He came fifth in grade one, fourth in grade two and third in grade three. He topped grades four and five. Apart from athletics, Alexio was hopeless at games.

When he completed grade five, he had no idea what he was going to do. Would Murimi send him to another school to do grade six and pay for his school fees? That was unlikely. Alexio was prepared to work for Murimi every holiday in return. Gomo? There was no chance. Maybe his mother could help? Would Gomo allow him to leave Makosa? The boy went home and told Murimi and Ruwa that he had passed his grade five examination. They did not seem particularly pleased. Alexio understood why later that evening when Murimi told Alexio that he should prepare to go back to Gomo at Makosa on the evening of the following day. Although Alexio didn't know what was going to happen, he was pleased to leave Murimi's home. Wherever he was going to go, he was not likely to be made to work as hard as he had been made to at Murimi's. Gomo could not really just let Alexio sit at Makosa. Many people hoped Gomo would send the boy to school; but they knew he wouldn't. If Gomo dared keep the boy at Makosa, he would have to put up with a lot of criticism.

Alexio began saying his goodbyes to his friends, elders and the villagers he had known since he came to live at Jena's village. He was sure he would see everybody again from time to time since he was only going to Makosa.

On the evening of the following day, he had an emotional parting with Ruwa. Murimi accompanied him to Makosa. They arrived at Gomo's *dare* and Alexio was formally 'returned' to Gomo.

'He is a man already, Gomo. He has a head. A good head. If I could, I would help him to go on with his schooling. A bright boy and a hard worker makes a good man. When you have discussed with him, let me know what he is going to do.' Murimi invited Alexio to come and stay whenever he wished. He thanked the boy and departed after a private talk with Gomo.

Two days after Alexio's arrival, Gomo summoned him into his hut. Gomo started by lavishly praising Alexio.

'Unfortunately, I can't do anything more for you. I would like to. But as you know, things are very difficult. Your younger brothers don't even have grade two. You have done very well. Now, you must think what you want do do. You are a man. You can make up your mind. But I think the most reasonable thing to do would be to go to Newton's farm and get a job there—Munda and Chipo would keep an eye on you should anything go wrong. You will not be on your own. As you know, I have no money. But here is something to use for your journey. I know it's not much but you will understand. Think about your plans and let me know.'

Gomo handed Alexio a one pound note.

Alexio respectfully accepted the one pound note and thanked Gomo for it.

'Father, would you keep the money for me until I am ready to leave? I am afraid I may lose it,' said the boy, stretching out his hand to give back the note to Gomo.

'Yes, of course,' answered Gomo, accepting the note, 'But Alexio, like a man, you must make your plans quickly. You must not waste too much time thinking about it. Let me know your plans by the day after tomorrow.' Gomo was always very firm when speaking to Alexio.

'Yes, father,' replied the boy humbly.

Why was Gomo in such a hurry to get rid of him? Alexio wondered.

'Is there anything you want to say to me or to ask me?'

Alexio was not used to being allowed to ask questions. Although he wanted to ask if Gomo would approve of a visit to Mtoko, he was afraid to ask. Asking a question like that could make Gomo change his mind about letting Alexio leave Makosa. Alexio said he did not have anything to say or any questions to ask.

When he came out of Gomo's hut, Alexio's mind was whirling with excitement. Excitement first, and then fear. He was going to see his mother again! Freely! He could stay with her for as long as he wanted! That was really wonderful. At last! But he had to hide his excitement. If Gomo got to know about Alexio's intention to go to Mtoko, he would not let the boy leave. Alexio was convinced of this. The most important thing he had to think about was what plans to tell Gomo. That plan should not mention anything about going to see his mother at all. Fear. Alexio was afraid Gomo could change his mind anytime. Gomo had made a suggestion, hadn't he? He had said that the best thing would be to go and join Chipo and Munda at Boss Newton's farm and find a job there. Well, what was the matter with that?

First, when was it best to leave? If he showed too much eagerness to leave, Gomo would be suspicious. But, on the other hand, Gomo seemed to want him to leave very quickly. Alexio could simply say he was leaving in two day's time. He would tell Gomo about it the next day. So he was to leave in three day's time. Then there was the question of travelling. Gomo would put him on a bus to Macheke. But the bus passed through Mtoko. He would have to get off there. And if Gomo decided to come with him as far as Mtoko to make sure Alexio would not get off the bus there, what was he going to do? He would get off the bus at the next village! No. Gomo would not succeed in preventing Alexio from seeing his mother. There was going to be some way of defeating any of Gomo's plans.

All right. Assuming he got to Mtoko, what next? If he stayed at Mtoko too long, Gomo would eventually hear about it. That would start problems for his mother . . . The real problem—the core of the problem—was what was he going to do? Alexio did not want to get a job. He wanted to go to school and do grade six. That was very clear in his mind. Where could he go to school? That wasn't a problem. He would have a chance in almost any school. His grade one examination result was very good. But where—at what place did he want to go and do grade six? That could be worked out later. Money was the biggest problem. Money for school fees and uniform. Where was it going to come from? Alexio was sure his mother could help. But she could not give him all the money he would need. He could work during the holidays. Plough or weed somebody's field. But would that raise enough money? He couldn't really decide anything before he talked to his mother. He was going to wait until he got to Mtoko and discuss everything with his mother.

As Alexio walked back into the village, he thought about how he would tell his uncle about his plans.

When Alexio arrived in the village, the sun was just setting. He picked up some logs for the fire at the *dare*. Gomo was not at the *dare* when Alexio arrived. He felt relieved. He lit the fire and sat down. Gomo's sons arrived and they all sat around until after the evening meal. Alexio stayed a short while and decided to go into the hut he was sharing with three of Gomo's sons and lie down. He began thinking about his future again.

Alexio was used to getting up very early. As on the first day since he arrived at Makosa from Jena's village, he woke up at the third crow of the cock. He lit the fire at the *dare* and waited for the others to wake up. It was a long wait. Under the light of a dying moon, he sat alone. The morning was very still. He was in the middle of his thoughts about the future when Gomo came out of his hut. He had come out to 'pass water'. He saw the glimmering fire at the *dare* and walked over there.

'Is that you, Alexio,' he asked as he came to the *dare*.

'Good morning, father. How did you sleep?'

'What are you doing up at this time of the night? Can't you sleep?'

'I am used to getting up early. That's all.'

'Is something the matter? Are you worried about something?' asked Gomo who, being naked, did not come too near to the boy.

'Nothing is the matter, father. At uncle Murimi's we would have done about two hour's work by now,' responded Alexio cheerfully.

'Alexio, are you upset because you are going to leave?'

'No, father—Well, just a little.'

'I'll go into the hut and get a blanket, I'll come back and we shall talk.'

Alexio became very worried. He wished he had remained inside the hut. Gomo came out wrapped in a blanket. Before sitting in his usual place, he placed some more logs on the fire.

'Alexio,' he began in a low and gentle voice, 'I want us to talk as man to man, my son. I don't want you to be afraid to tell me what you feel and what you think, I want you to feel free with me . . . You hear?'

'Yes, father. But I have always been free with you.'

'We will never have a good relationship unless we tell each other what we think. You agree?'

'Yes, father.'

'I am very proud of you. Maybe you don't know that. You have done very well throughout your schooling here at Makosa. I have not been able to give you what I would have wanted to give you. You know how poor we are. You know that many people in the village like you. They know you are a hard worker. They know you are competent. They know you are obedient. You know that they like you for many reasons. You are respectful and polite to them . . . You may think I have been very hard with you. But I wanted you, my brother's son, to grow into the man you are now. Nobody can take away what you have. Not even me. I don't want you to leave home with bitterness. Think about it. Are you not proud of coming top of your class? Are you not proud for being admired by so many people? . . . Alexio?'

'Yes, father. I am.'

'All I am saying to you is if all that has happened to you had not happened—if I and your uncle Murimi had been soft with you—would you be the boy you are now?'

'No, father.'

'Well, I don't think you would be. Of course, you can now think what you like, but everything I have done was meant to help you. If when you go, you want to forget us here, you can. But the spirits of the ancestors will watch you . . . You say something.'

'I think all you have said is very true. But I think you are mistaken if you think I am going to forget you. How can a man forget his family?'

'You are a wise boy, Alexio. Very wise indeed. Have you made your plans yet?—if you haven't, don't worry. I am not trying to hurry you. But if you have, I would very much like to know them.' There were tears in Gomo's voice. Alexio felt above Gomo. The boy didn't know what to say to his uncle.

'Alexio, I have thought about selling a cow to send you to do grade six. It's true I have. But I would sell one for your grade six, another for grade seven and a third for grade eight. Wouldn't I? That's just you. How about your younger brothers? You know Rudo and Chipo don't send me anything anymore. Rudo is buying a house in Highfields. I don't know what for. A woman buying a house! She has become a man. That is my fault too. Chipo and her husbånd have his family and their own children to support. Alexio what can I hold on to?'

Alexio decided it was best to talk about his plans while Gomo was in that mood.

'Father, I have made my plans.'

'Ah. Let's hear them, Alexio. Let's hear them.'

'I would like to leave on today's bus.'

'Today's bus? But you haven't prepared for the journey.'

'All I need is to wash my two shirts and my two pairs of short trousers. I can go to the river and wash them now. I will bathe while they dry.'

'I still don't know where you are going.'

'From here I want to go to Mtoko. Maybe I can spend a week there. I am sure mother can add a little money to what you have given me already. From Mtoko, I should travel to Salisbury. I have heard that if someone has a house in the townships in Salisbury, their children or relatives can go to a government school. People don't have to pay as much in school fees as at a mission school. I know that mother has a brother who lives in Salisbury. Maybe he would agree to let me live with him and his family so that I can go to school.'

'Well, I don't want to dissuade you. But you realize that your mother's brother may not want to take the responsibility. If this plan doesn't work, what are you going to do? Alexio,

Rudo has already done much for you. It would not be reasonable to ask her to help you again. So if you go to Salisbury, don't expect Rudo to help you.'

'I understand, father. I don't want Rudo to do anything for me. If you are afraid that I will ask her, I won't even visit her in Salisbury.'

'So what are you going to do if this plan does not work.'

'I think I will get a job and do grade six by correspondence.'

'Well, as I said, I don't think this is a good plan. But I don't want to stand in your way. I would have thought you would take this chance to get yourself a job. With grade five, you will get a good job on a farm. You can earn yourself some money and buy yourself some clothes. You will be independent.'

The sun was just about to rise. Gomo stood up to go into his hut to get dressed. Before he left, he told Alexio:

'You had better run to the river and wash your clothes, otherwise they will not dry in time. The bus passes early these days. If I were you I would walk to Mtoko and save a few shillings. You might arrive at Mtoko and discover that your mother does not have any money. But anyway, do as you please.'

As soon as Gomo disappeared into his hut, Alexio jumped up! He was elated. He rushed into his sleeping-hut and picked up his spare shirt and pair of trousers. When he came out of the hut, he was ready to sprint down to the river but Gomo was calling him. Alexio felt weak in the knees as he went to Gomo. Had something gone wrong already? Why! Why! Why had he talked to Gomo in that way? It would have been better to stick to the original plan! Gomo was standing in front of his hut.

'Here is some soap, my son. Hurry, otherwise you are going to miss your bus . . .'

Alexio felt as light as an autumn leaf as he ran down to the river. He was so happy. He decided to forgive Gomo for everything! He wondered how he had managed to talk to Gomo the way he had done.

At that time of the morning the water in the river was still cold. He washed his spare clothes which were his best clothes first. Then he undressed and washed the second pair. Then he bathed. To think that by that afternoon, he would be with his mother! The best thing about it was that she didn't even know that he would be arriving! Happy thoughts raced through his mind. This was the beginning of many good things, he thought. He would enjoy saying goodbye to many people. It was so much better to just say he was leaving that day rather than tomorrow or the day after. That way he was sure to say goodbye only once. Some people would just hear about it: 'Alexio left today'. He would keep them posted about what he was doing. Joyce! Joyce was one person he had to see before he left. It would be sad to leave Joyce but he was sure he would see her again. He would write to her as often as possible.

Alexio, now twelve years old, was a year younger than Joyce. Their 'affair' had started some five years earlier. It started one day after Sunday School. Joyce had come up to Alexio and handed the man a folded paper out of an arithmetic exercise-book. On it had been written the words 'I LOVE YOU'. The note had not been signed. Soon after delivering the note, Joyce had run off. Other children had seen all this. They had wrestled Alexio and read his note. From that day, Alexio had been Joyce's 'husband' and Joyce, Alexio's 'wife'. Alexio had been very annoyed by these labels. In fact, he had even fought for being labelled 'Joyce's husband'. Even Joyce's mother addressed him as her 'son-in-law'. In the end Alexio ignored both Joyce and the labels.

Joyce was tall, slim and slightly bow-legged. People used to joke about her bow-legs and her hair. Joyce's hair was longer than most little girls'. People used to say Joyce was so thin because all the goodness of the food she ate was taken up by her hair. It was her nose that mainly made Alexio dislike her. It wasn't its shape or anything like that. She just seemed to have a perpetually runny nose.

Then came the time when she went to visit her brother and sister-in-law in Salisbury during a school holiday. When she came back, the water of the city and the soap had agreed with her very well. She was very different. All the little boys were after her. On the first day at school after the holidays, she brought Alexio sweets and biscuits which she had saved for him. Alexio had not only begun to take interest but also to assert himself. If anyone 'molested' Joyce, they were asking for a fight with Alexio. That stage of the relationship came to an end. Joyce had been one class behind Alexio. When they both began to top their classes the children below them began to treat them differently—with some sort of respect. Joyce began a relationship based on their academic interest. By the time Joyce was in grade four and Alexio was in grade five, a very open friendship had developed between the two children.

Alexio bathed while waiting for his clothes to dry. They were still damp when he decided to get dressed and start back into the village. It was best to pass through Joyce's father's huts and say goodbye. He hoped she would be there. He thought he would be ashamed to be seen in damp unironed clothes. But he dismissed the thought. It was not important.

He rushed to Joyce's home and saw her mother first.

'Why, my son-in-law is in a terrible hurry. Are you going somewhere?—by the way I haven't seen you since you passed your grade five. They all say you did very well. Congratulations! We knew you would do well.'

'Thank you very much—is Joyce about?'

'Joyce! Joyce! Come out! Your man is here! . . . Now that you have finished, what are you going to do?'

'I am leaving today—'

'Today?!'

'Yes. I am going to see my mother first. Then to Salisbury. I may be able to do grade six there.'

'By the spirits of the ancestors! I am so thankful. So grateful!' Joyce's mother shouted with emotional delight.

Joyce came out and laughed at her mother's excitement.

'What's the matter with you mother?' Joyce asked.

'Now you can forget all of them, Alexio. Especially Gomo. Forget the rest of us! But not my daughter! You hear Alexio?'

'I won't forget anyone, Ma Tombi. Why should I forget anyone?'

'If you ever do forget her, the spirits of the ancestors will strike you. Now, you speak with Joy.'

'Joy, I have come to say goodbye.'

'Goodbye?!'

'I am going to Mtoko on the bus today.'

'When are you coming back?'

'I don't know. I am going to Salisbury from there.'

'Salisbury!'

'I may live with my mother's brother and go to school there.'

'Lucky you! There is not much time before the bus comes—Go and prepare for your journey. I will come and see you off. Let us meet at the bus. Be early,' said Joyce.

'Well, Ma Tombi, remain well. I am sure I shall be coming back. So I shall see you again. Could you convey my farewell to Joyce's father and everyone.' Alexio was now very nervous. The sun was quite high up. He hurried to Gomo's huts.

'If you see my son and his family in Salisbury, greet him for us! Don't forget to tell them you didn't inform us about your departure in time otherwise we would have sent them something!! You hear, Alexio,' Ma Tombi shouted behind him.

'Yes! I will!' he shouted.

Alexio bade anyone he met on the way, good morning and said goodbye. At Gomo's huts, the whole family was waiting for him. They all looked so sad. It was as though they were losing him forever. The children didn't know what to say. They simply stood around him. Ma Rudo came and told Alexio:

'Tell your mother to come and visit us soon. She might have some seeds that I need. Tell her if I find someone going to Mtoko, and returing to Makosa, I will ask them to see her and bring the seeds back for me. To Rudo, tell her I have not been too well. When she is given leave, she must come home. It's easier for her to come here than for us to go to the city. The old dress she sent last time is already worn out, as you can see. If she can't send a dress, ask her to just send some rags to mend the dress with.'

Gomo was next to say something:

'I hope you will remain the same. If things work out well with your uncle, send me a word. The most important thing, Alexio, is to keep us informed about yourself. Tell Tendayi that I may be visiting Mtoko in a month or two. I shall see her then . . . Well, you had better go for your bus. Your brothers and sisters will accompany you . . . Have a good journey. Don't forget us . . .'

He gave Alexio the one pound note and an extra two shillings and six pence. Gomo and Alexio shook hands. Alexio's small bundle of his spare clothes was carried by one of Gomo's sons. The party, consisting of nine children, left for the bus-stop. Alexio was on the verge of crying. He felt so sorry for Gomo. He didn't feel any hate for him now. He also felt sorry for the children who were accompanying him. He felt sorry to be leaving. Maybe he shouldn't be going? The thought crossed his mind. But that was impossible. He knew he had to go. Joyce. Thinking about Joyce finally brought the tears down. 'You have to be strong—stronger than that!' he thought as he smiled and wiped the tears off his face.

The bus was already there when they got to the bus-stop. There were many people standing around. Only three or four were actually catching the bus. Some people were there to send their vegetables or fruit to be sold in Salisbury. Two women and one man were there to send messages to their children via the conductor and the driver of the bus. A few young boys and a few women and a man were trying to sell everything from sugar cane to boiled eggs to the passengers. But business was not good. Most of the people just stood around and looked at the bus, the people inside, and each other. For most, arrival and departure of the bus were the main events of the day.

Joyce was already at the bus-stop. Alexio walked up to her.

'Joy, I will write to you when I arrive at Mtoko. Then I will write you again after I have spent about a week in Salisbury. I hope you will reply.'

'Of course I will reply. But only if you write. I won't know your address. There is really nothing to say to you right now. You know what you are doing. I just hope everything will work out for you.'

The other children were standing around Alexio and Joyce. An old man walked up to the group and asked who was travelling.

'Alexio,' the children answered in a chorus. That was the final moment. The bus driver started the engine.

'Well, goodbye,' said Alexio addressing Joyce more than anyone else. The children surged forward and shook hands with him. Those who couldn't shake hands with him simply touched him on the shoulders and on the arms.

Getting on the bus was a fight. It was already full up.

'Move to the back! Move to the back!' the conductor, who was still outside, kept on shouting. The bus began to move. The door was still open and the conductor had now managed to put one foot on the first of the steps of the bus. Alexio was surrounded by taller people. With one hand gripping a bar and the other his bundle, he tried to keep his head up in order to breathe properly. Everyone swayed to and fro. The people at his back were pushing forward. The bus began to pick up speed. Inch by inch, people moved towards the back of the bus. When Alexio was about half-way from the back of the bus, he tried to find a place to put down his bundle. But he did not have very much luck. Under the seat on his right was a goat tied to a string held by one of the three men sitting on the seat meant for two. He couldn't see what was under the seat on the left row but he heard the sound of chickens from under there. Under the second seat, there was a short bundle of sugar cane. By now the bus was travelling at full speed. From the door-side top of the bus came heavy tapping. The conductor who had closed the door, swung it open. A foot appeared on top of the door and the conductor's assistant, who had been arranging the luggage on top of the bus, climbed in. How dangerous it was!

When the bus came to the next village, it stopped. One old woman got off and three men got in. Now Alexio was sticky with sweat. The air inside the bus smelt of sweat. Many people were talking very loudly. The bus started to move again. It stopped at every village until it came to Mtoko. Despite being so crowded, there was a lot of good humour in the bus throughout the journey.

Alexio got off the bus and made his way to his mother's huts. As on his previous visit, he was sighted a distance away from the village. Children raced to meet him. Some remembered him, others didn't. They carried his bundle and told him about what had recently been happening in the village. His grandmother, his mother's mother had died the week before. An uncle and his family and their old battered car were in the village on a visit from Salisbury. So and so had passed this or that examination at school. And so and so had failed. A niece was pregnant and nobody knew who was responsible etc, etc.

When Alexio arrived at the huts, he got a message from a little boy that his mother's brother wanted to see him immediately. Alexio walked into his uncle's hut. The group of children, men and women who had greeted him and walked with him, remained outside his uncle's hut. After exchanging greetings, his uncle asked him if he had run away again. No, he had not. That was all his uncle wanted to know. Alexio proceeded to his mother's hut.

As on the previous occasion, word of Alexio's arrival had filtered through to his mother. She found herself wondering whether Alexio had run away again. The meeting between mother and son was, unlike the previous occasion, very emotional. Tendayi hugged her son and pressed him closely to her body. When they had finished greeting each other, Tendayi asked her son:

'You haven't run away again, have you?'

'Not this time, mother. No.'

'What? You mean Gomo simply let you leave?'

'Yes, mother.'

Tendayi doubted what her son was saying. There had to be a reason for Gomo to let Alexio leave Makosa. She could not imagine what it could be. But as Alexio gave her more news of himself, she began to see why Gomo had allowed the boy to leave. Mother and son had many things to say to each other. Tendayi cooked a special meal of *sadza* and chicken. They talked over the meal and soon arrived at the problem of Alexio's future.

'I agree with you, I agree very much. You must go to school. If I had known that this would happen, I would have spent all these years saving a little here and a little there. But who was to know? As it is, I just can't help you, my child. I still can't believe it. Gomo just letting you leave like that!'

'Mother, what do you think I should do?'

'You are talking about going to school, aren't you?'

'Yes mother.'

'Well, as I was saying, everything is happening very unexpectedly. But you will be here for sometime, won't you? We will think of something. You haven't even sat down, so to speak. Things will take a little time.'

'Mother, all I want to know is whether you see how you can help or not. That's all I want to know.'

'That's what I am trying to tell you. We have to see what we can do.'

'Which is what?'

'If I say I can't see what I can do at the moment, what does that give you? We must take time and think over the possibilities. You must not be so impatient.'

'So this really means you can't help?' Alexio asked.

'Alexio, my child, if I say I can't help you, what can you do? You are still too young—'

'Mother, if you can't help me, I can make my own plans. You must not treat me like a child.'

'But what are you? What are you but a child?' The argument escalated and went on for a long time.

'Well, I am quite capable of doing everthing for myself. I don't need your help. I have seen you enough. I am leaving for Salisbury tomorrow.'

'If you can, go. But you are mistaken to think you can just do what you like.

As usual Alexio woke up early the next morning. When his mother woke up, she asked him what he wanted to do with his day.

'Mother, I told you yesterday. I am leaving for Salisbury today.'

'Now, now, Alexio. You are really being childish. You have no patience at all.'

'Mother, if you want to help, I need some extra money.'

'Alexio, if you are going to do things your way, I can't help.'

'Thank you, mother. Goodbye, I will see you again some time soon.'

Alexio said goodbye to his uncle and the whole family. Most of them expected to see him back before the afternoon. But Alexio walked to the shops where the buses stopped. There he caught a bus for Salisbury.

When Alexio got off the bus at Harare Musika, he didn't know where to go. At first this did not worry him. The splendour of the city totally absorbed him. The Salisbury he had imagined and had tried to recall from the time he had lived with Rudo, was very different from what he now saw. After happily wandering about aimlessly he remembered that Gomo had said Rudo was buying a house in Highfields. He decided to go to Highfields. Nearly all his money had gone on his bus fare. He asked for directions to Highfields and began walking there. No, he did not want to see Rudo. Just where she lived. Highfields turned out to be much further than he had thought. But there were many things to see. Enough not to make him think about where he was going to sleep that night or what he was going to eat. There was no question of going back to Mtoko. Besides not having the money to get back, he could not face having his mother saying to him: 'I told you'.

In Highfields, Alexio wandered until it was dark. Then he decided that he would have to find Rudo.

'I am looking for my sister called Rudo Shonga. Do you know her?' Most people's first reaction was to laugh. Then they generally replied that Highfields was a big place.

'Do you know if she lives in Old Highfields or New Highfields?' asked one stranger.

'No, I don't know. All I know is that she is buying a house here.'

'It's more likely to be New Highfields then. But even New Highfields has many sections. Egypt, Engineering, Canaan, Lusaka and so on. She could be in any of these sections.'

If he was going to find Rudo, Alexio realized, it would take days. And what would he do in the meantime. The main shopping centre in Highfields was called Machipisa. Alexio, like a stray cat found himself there. Most of the shops were closed but electric lights were on. The boy wandered around the centre until he heard someone playing a flute. He walked

towards where the music was. He saw a group of boys
gathered outside. The music was good. Should he go there or
not? He was a little afraid. These boys could beat him up. He
had heard that boys in towns didn't need any reason to beat
up someone. Alexio slowly walked towards where the boys
were. The nearer he got to them, the more slowly he walked.
Finally, he came to where the boys were and stopped. Most of
them were wearing tight fitting jeans or trousers and pointed
shoes. The collars of their shirts were up. Their hair was very
neatly combed out. Alexio felt very out of place in his khaki
clothes and bare feet. What was he doing there? He was
standing behind the boys who were watching another
boy playing the flute. Two boys were jiving to the music. A few
of the boys were smoking. Alexio wanted to move away but he
was afraid. He was afraid someone would notice him. He
didn't want to be noticed. Then abruptly the music came to
an end. The boys clapped their hands and were praising the
boy who had been playing the flute. To Alexio, everybody
seemed to be talking to everybody else. They were all calling
each other 'sonny'. Then came some music, this time from a
radio. The radio was inside the cafe but there was a big
speaker over the doorway. All the boys started jiving. Alexio
decided to move on.

'Hey sonny, do you have a cigarette?' said someone from
behind. Alexio did not realize the someone was talking to
him. He continued walking away. Then a hand grabbed him
by the collar of his khaki shirt.

'Don't you know that it's rude not to answer when you are
being spoken to?'

Alexio was very scared. He was sure he was going to be
beaten up. Alexio was now facing a boy who could not have
been much older than him. The boy was taller than Alexio.

'I'm really sorry, I didn't know you were talking to me.
Please forgive me. I don't smoke.'

'Which "reserve" are you from?'

'Makosa. I come from Makosa.'

The boy took his hand off Alexio.

'Do you live in Engineering?' asked the boy.

'Where is Engineering?' asked Alexio.

'Where you are right now. Have you only just arrived?'

'Yes. Today.'

'You are lost, aren't you? Do you know where you are staying?'

'Well, I am looking for my sister. She has a house in Highfields. But I don't know which section she lives in.'

'Do you know the number?'

'No'

'Jesus! And you think you will find her?'

'I hope so.'

'Does she know you are arriving today?'

'No'

'Have you ran away from home?'

'No'

'This is madness. A kid like you wandering about like this!'

Alexio felt annoyed by this but decided to let it pass.

'Where are you going to sleep tonight?'

'I will find somewhere.'

'What's your name?'

'Alexio'

The boy's name was Sam.

That night Sam took Alexio home. Home for Sam was a lodger's room in a house not far from Machipisa shopping centre. Sam lived in the room with his grandmother—his mother's mother. When Alexio saw her, she reminded him of Ma Munda. She was big, round and full of warmth.

'Mbuya, this is a friend of mine called Alexio.'

'Welcome, Alexio. Have you boys eaten?'

Sam answered: 'No Mbuya. We are very hungry.'

'Then why do you stay out so late? You know Sam, that I have to get up early to go to the market. Take that primus stove outside and fill it with paraffin.'

'Alexio, you see what these modern wives are like. Complain, complain is all they ever do,' said Sam in humour and took the primus stove and a gallon-tin of paraffin outside.

'Where do you live, Alexio?' asked Mbuya.

'I come from Makosa's village.'

'No. I mean in Highfields.'

'I have only just arrived from home and I am looking for my

sister, but I haven't found her yet?'

'You mean you are here on your own?'

'Well, yes. But I should be able to find my sister tomorrow.'

'The courage you children today have never ceases to surprise me. You are just like Sam. He has suffered very much. He has had to look after himself since he was very young. Suffering has—'

'She is telling lies, Alexio. I married her the day I was born. We have been very happy since that day. She is the best wife in the world. Her daughter met this young man while she was already pregnant. The young man told the daughter to go and throw me into Mukuwisi River on the day I was born. Otherwise he was not going to marry her.'

Alexio liked very much the way Sam spoke to his grandmother. He wished he had a grandmother like that. Alexio could never dare talk like that to anyone as old as Mbuya. But she didn't seem to mind at all. Alexio was respectful and polite to Mbuya.

'You see, Alexio here, is a really well-brought up boy. You can see for yourself the difference between you "location-born" children and the children from the "reserves".' She was addressing her 'man'.

'I don't feel at all jealous Mbuya. You don't have to divorce me either. If you marry Alexio and keep me, you will have the best of both worlds. Think about it. How many women are so lucky?'

Mbuya chuckled. It was obvious that she loved and enjoyed her grandson very much. She served them the meal: beef stew with spring onions, tomatoes and greens with *sadza*. Sam talked all the time. Alexio had been brought up never to talk over a meal. He was fascinated by Sam's city way of speaking. He seemed to have a great deal of knowledge about almost everything under the sun. Sam had also just passed his grade five. He would definitely be continuing with his studies at the same school.

Mbuya climbed into her junk-yard double-bed which occupied more than a quarter of the room.

'Alexio, eat your food. Don't take notice of what Sam is saying. He never lets a fly settle on his lips. I am going to sleep. Sam, you will take Alexio to the Superintendant's office and try to find Rudo's house tomorrow. Alexio, whether you find Rudo or not, this is your home. I will leave two shillings and six pence for each of you before I leave in the morning . . . Don't forget to put the candle out before you go to sleep.'

Alexio thanked her and felt very grateful. Sam asked Alexio if he wanted to go out to visit some friends. Alexio said he didn't mind but Mbuya, who was trying to doze off, objected.

'Alexio has just arrived and must be very tired. Not tonight, Sam.'

'Stop interfering, Mbuya. Why don't you just go to sleep. Alexio can answer for himself.'

Alexio felt very embarrassed. He thought Sam was being a little too rude.

'Actually, I am quite tired. We can meet your friends tomorrow,' said Alexio.

Sam and Alexio finished eating. They talked for a bit before taking a blanket each from under Mbuya's bed. They slept on the floor. Alexio tried to think about what was happening but he was too tired and soon fell asleep.

When he woke up the next morning, Mbuya had already left and Sam was not in the room. A saucepan of boiling water was steaming away on the primus stove. Alexio wanted to turn off the primus stove but didn't know how to do it. He wanted to add some cold water to the saucepan but didn't know where to get the water from either. He was just about to remove the saucepan from the primus stove when Sam walked in.

'Did you sleep well?' asked Sam.

'Very well. And you?'

'Fine. Let me show you some of these things so that you can do them for yourself.'

Sam poured some water from the saucepan into the dish. He carried it out of the room and they walked to the back of the house. There was a very small brick hut a few yards from the house. It was the toilet and shower room, Sam explained.

'As you can see, the houses are arranged in rows of two. This path between the back of the houses is called a sanitary lane.' Sam placed the dish under a water-tap on the outside of the toilet.

'What's that watch for?' Alexio asked, pointing to a meter fixed to the water pipe.

'That's for measuring how much water we use. We have to pay for it at the end of each month.'

'Pay for water!' exclaimed Alexio.

'Soon there will be electricity in all the houses in New Highfields and we will have to pay for that too.' Sam ran some cold water into the dish and gave Alexio a small towel and some soap.

'The toilet. When you have finished using it, you just pull the chain like this,' said Sam flushing the toilet. Sam walked back to the room. When Alexio returned to the room, Sam had made some tea and was spreading margarine on sliced bread.

'We won't be eating lunch, so eat as much as possible.' After their meal, the two new friends wandered around Highfields with Sam showing Alexio the place. They went to Machipisa and visited the market. Mbuya was there. She ran a vegetable stall. They talked to her for a while before heading to the Superintendant's office.

At the Superintendant's office, they got Rudo's address. Sam casually informed Alexio that Rudo lived only two streets away from where Sam lived. Alexio couldn't wait to go to Rudo's house. But when they got there, there was nobody at the house. She was at work. They went back to Sam's house and ate some more bread and drank tea. They talked about everything: their families, school, girls and even the future. There was no doubt that a new friendship had been born.

Sam decided that they should go to Rudo's house and leave a message. Rudo would come to Sam's house when she returned from work. Sam and Alexio took a walk to Old Highfields. Sam pointed out and explained many things. Alexio asked many questions and learned a lot.

Mbuya was preparing the evening meal when there was a knock on the door. They all knew it was Rudo. Sam opened the door and let her in.

'My child! My child!' cried Rudo as she embraced Alexio. The greetings went on for a while. It was a very emotional and happy reunion for Alexio and Rudo. Rudo thanked Mbuya for looking after Alexio. Rudo wanted to take Alexio home, but Mbuya insisted that he stayed for supper and asked Rudo to join them for the meal. But Rudo could not stay long because she had food cooking on the stove at her house. Besides, she had to cook for her 'husband'. Mbuya insisted that Alexio stay. Sam would accompany him after the meal. Rudo took the small bundle containing Alexio's shirt and short trousers and his grade five certificate, all of which were wrapped in brown paper. She left. Mbuya asked Alexio to talk about the time he had lived with Rudo. Alexio told her the little he could remember. She told him where she lived, what she was doing, how old Sam was and other things at that time. After eating, the boys left for Rudo's house.

Unlike Mbuya, Rudo lived in her own house. All the houses in New Highfields were more or less identical. Each house had a kitchen, a sitting/dining room, a bedroom and a spare room with its own front door. Most house-owners let the spare room. The spare room brought in little, but much needed, extra cash to help pay for the lease. Rudo had another meal ready for Alexio and Sam when they arrived. There was a man sitting on one of the two sofas in Rudo's sitting-room. His name was Tauya. He and Rudo had lived together for about four years. Alexio had never heard about Tauya before. They all sat and ate at the table. Sam, a very sensitive boy, did not stay long after the meal. He knew that Rudo and Alexio had many things to talk about. Sam said he would come to see Alexio the next morning.

After Sam left, Alexio told Rudo and Tauya about his problems and about wanting to go to school.

'You are still my child, Alexio. You have come home. But there are a few things you have to understand. I am your mother and Tauya here, is your father. You must give him respect. I get on well with Tendayi, your mother, but I don't want too much involvement with her. She abandoned you when you were only three. It pains my heart to think of it. You can go and see her from time to time. To avoid any problems with my father, every school holiday you should go home and help as much as possible at the fields. I know he is going to object to my having you here. But I know how to make him accept it.'

Rudo went on talking but Alexio didn't listen to her anymore. He was going to be able to continue with school! That was all that mattered in the world! He felt so happy.

After the long talk, Rudo took Alexio to the spare room.

'This is your room. Both Tauya and I leave for work early.' She gave him the keys to his own room and the back door of the house. She told him never to leave the house unlocked. She gave him some money to buy food and firewood. He would give himself lunch but Rudo would cook the evening meal when she came back from work. She took Alexio into the kitchen and showed him where everything that he would need was.

Alexio went to bed very late that night. He had asked Rudo for some paper and a pen to write letters. Rudo gave him some stamps. First, Alexio wrote to his mother. He apologized for the way in which he had left Mtoko. He told her everything Rudo had said. He would visit her every school holiday before going to Makosa or on his way from Makosa to Salisbury. Finally, he asked her to write to him as often as possible. Rudo had told him not to write to Gomo until she had done so first. His second letter was to Joy. He told her everything and warned her not to say anything to anyone until Gomo had been informed of the arrangement by Rudo. He thought about his new friend Sam. Alexio thought how lucky he had been.

Rudo and Tauya sought and got a place for Alexio at Sam's school. Rudo and Tauya took Alexio into town one Saturday afternoon and bought him some clothes and some shoes. Alexio's life with Tauya and Rudo began to follow a routine. He got up just after Rudo and Tauya had left for work. He cleaned the house, did the washing-up and gave himself breakfast—usually porridge, bread with margarine and tea. On school days he popped over to Sam's house. They walked to school together. At lunch time, Sam and Alexio came back home and had some more bread and tea, at Rudo's house first and then Mbuya's, before returning to school. After school, late in the afternoon, Alexio watered the vegetables in the yard or weeded. He went to Machipisa and did any shopping that was necessary. At the beginning, he laid out everything for supper so that when Rudo got home, she would do nothing but cook. Rudo had taught Alexio to cook. While waiting for Tauya and Rudo, he did his homework or talked to Sam. Once a week, Alexio helped by washing and ironing Rudo and Tauya's clothes. Rudo and Tauya gave him a little pocket money whenever there was some to spare.

Sam and Alexio were not surprised to find themselves in the same class. They both had very good grade five examination results. There were three classes of grade six at the school. These were divided according to academic ability. At the end of each term and in the final grade six examinations Sam was at the top of the class. Alexio came second throughout that year. In fact, this pattern remained the same in grade seven and in grade eight.

Over the next three years, through the influence of Rudo and Tauya, reading the newspapers, attending public political meetings, Sam and Alexio developed a very strong appetite for politics. They discussed the everyday problems that faced the black people not just in the cities but in the whole country. There was a political movement called the African Party at that time. It stood for very modest aims: the end of racial discrimination, the right for black people to vote, participation in government, realistic wages for workers, more schools and hospitals in African areas and so on. But the white government never listened to the Party. Sam and Alexio spent hours and hours discussing the means by which the Party could realize its aims. They understood and supported the aims of the Party but after sometime they became very disillusioned by the lack of any credible plan by the Party to realize its aims. Alexio and Sam also used to argue with Tauya and Rudo, who were both officials in the Party, over the Party's lack of plans.

One Saturday, Tauya and Rudo left for work at about five-thirty as usual. They preferred to leave for work at that time because there wasn't much traffic going into the city. At that time of the morning, the road from Highfields into the city was relatively quiet. It was knotted with small groups of workers—mainly domestic servants—walking to work in white suburbs such as Southerton, Waterfalls, Avondale,

Greendale, and other parts of the city even as far away as
Highlands. Cyclists were few. There were hardly any cars or
buses yet. However, an hour or so later, the road would be a
solid train of pedestrians, cyclists of all kinds, cars—mainly
old battered ones, and jam-packed buses. The pedestrians
would be ceaselessly cursing the cyclists who would be trying
to drive the pedestrians into the ditches. The cyclists would be
cursing the pedestrians and car- and bus-drivers. The drivers
would be swearing, hooting and blazing their lights. Fatal
accidents were of common occurrence on that road.
Everybody regarded everybody else as being in their way.
Tempers were quick and short but deep down inside, they all
knew they were all on the same journey for the same
reason—to survive.

On this Saturday morning, Tauya who didn't have to start
work until eight-thirty, rode with Rudo out of the city towards
Highlands, before he returned to Manica Road where he
worked for a Dr Harper. He was the messenger, the 'tea-boy'
and the general dog's body in the doctor's third-floor surgery.
The surgery was housed in a white Victorian building located
about half-way up Manica Road. Here Tauya had worked
since he was sixteen years old. From his pear-shaped brown
face, it was hard to tell that he was now forty-three years of
age. They thought highly of him and trusted him at Dr
Harper's surgery. Some years previously, they had, as a sign
of respect for him, ceased calling him 'boy'. They now
addressed him as Tauya. They had even entrusted him with a
key to the surgery so that he could clean and tidy up before
the working day started.

When he got to work, Tauya parked his bicycle in the usual
place, against a wall in the backyard. Out of his short-sleeved
shirt, he took a packet of 'Star' cigarettes and lit one. He, as
an African, was not allowed to smoke inside the building;
nobody was allowed to smoke in the surgery. After smoking
half his cigarette, he stubbed it out and replaced the
remainder in the packet. He walked up the stairs. Again,
although there was a lift, it was not for use by Africans. A big
sign outside the lift clearly stated so. Tauya let himself into
the surgery, gathered his cleaning materials and began by

scrubbing the floors.

In Highlands, Rudo's day began much as usual. She made Madam her usual morning cup of tea and went on with her usual Saturday morning chores. Boss Koopman, the gentleman who used to spend some nights at Madam's house when Rudo first came to work there, had moved into Madam's house some two and a half years previously. Neither he nor Madam worked on Saturdays, Master Peter and Master John had no school on Saturdays either.

The family always had their breakfast a little later at weekends. Like other families, they had their conversations over meals. This morning's breakfast conversation turned out to be mildly serious. The subject was whether the children should or should not speak to Rudo with some politeness. Madam believed that although being polite to Rudo was not important, the children should be polite in order to get into the habit of being respectful.

Master Peter did not agree:

'For my part, I would never make such a stupid mistake. I mean confusing manners towards Rudo and "people" is rather like confusing black and white—I mean the colours.'

'John may have that problem but I shouldn't think he will grow up with it because he is quite clever.'

'I don't have any problem of the sort,' Master John said, 'Anyway if I had my way, I would fire Rudo.'

'Why, John? Rudo has been very good and kind to you.'

'She wants all white people to be killed. I saw it in an African newspaper. My friend at school, Joseph brought it. I saw her picture and her name in the newspaper.'

'Are you sure, John?' asked Boss.

'I can call Joseph and ask him to give me that newspaper.'

True. Rudo's picture had appeared in the *Daily News* two weeks earlier. It showed her addressing a public meeting in Highfields. The caption, under the picture read: 'Do we have to kill all the white people in this country before we can be heard?'

Master John telephoned Joseph who promised to ride over on his bicycle and bring the paper. An hour later, Joseph arrived with the paper.

had never thought about the life Rudo led
of employment. Madam was shocked to
s political. Nothing in the black woman's
uld have led Madam to believe Rudo could be an
can nationalist. Madam was about to go and
Rudo with the newspaper when Boss had a better

'You are going to fire her, aren't you?' asked Boss.

'This very minute!'

'Women! Always emotional,' said Boss forcing a laugh, 'I'll tell you what? She deserves more punishment for all this.' He explained the punishment to Madam and Madam rather liked the idea.

Rudo was allowed Saturday afternoons and Sundays off except on a few occasions such as when there was a party at the house. Every Saturday afternoon before she was dismissed, Rudo was presented with a small parcel as a present. Usually, it was an assortment of weekly left-overs from the fridge.

On this Saturday, Madam came to dismiss Rudo.

'Sorry, Rudo. I haven't got much for you today,' said Madam pressing a small brown bag into Rudo's hands.

'Madam, I don't expect anything at all. This here is something. Thank you very much,' Rudo replied in her usual humble way.

'Oh, you are sweet, Rudo. Now, I want you to listen to me carefully. This parcel is for you and your man only. Understand?'

'Yes, Madam,' responded Rudo apprehensively. She didn't look at what she was given in front of Madam.

'Do not drink it with anybody. You tell nobody else I give you this. Do you understand, Rudo?'

'Yes, Madam. I promise. Thank you, Madam.'

'If police catch you with this, you and your boy go to jail long long time. Understand? Alright, you may go now. But be careful, okay.'

'Good weekend to you, Madam.'

'Same to you! see you on Monday!'

Rudo walked out of the house and tucked her present into

the laundry basket on the carrier of her bicycle. The basket was full of clothes and sheets she had to iron over the weekend. She pushed her bicycle out of the yard and left by her usual way at the rear of the house. Behind the shack which was her house until she moved out to Highfields, she leaned the bicycle against the wall and satisfied her curiosity. Madam had given her a small bottle of gin. She was very pleased, but she also knew Africans were not allowed to drink spirits. She would be careful. After all Madam had warned her.

When she arrived home, she was exhausted. Tauya gave her some bread and tea. Alexio had gone to a youth meeting of the Party with Sam. Rudo and Tauya sat down and opened the bottle of gin.

About half an hour after Rudo and Tauya took the first sips of their afternoon drinks, Sam and Alexio arrived at the house.

'You have never told me about this rich relative of yours,' Sam said to Alexio.

'What rich relative?'

'The one who owns that grey Austin Westminster parked in front of your house.'

'It may be somebody who has just parked it there and gone off into any of these houses.'

'Alexio, sometimes you are so stupid I just can't believe it. That is an unmarked police car! All I was asking you is why should they be around.'

When the two boys tried to enter the house, the door was bolted from the inside. They knocked and the door was opened. A short and fat black man with blood-shot eyes opened the door.

'What do you want?' he demanded.

'They are bad times when people have to be asked what they want in their own house,' said Sam trying to push past the black policeman. Alexio was behind Sam. Rudo's cousin was a little scared as this was the first time he had ever been near a policeman. Policemen were people to be scared of: Alexio had heard too many stories of their brutality.

'Let them in,' ordered a white detective who was inside the house.

In the sitting-room, Tauya and Rudo, each with both hands handcuffed, were standing on the far side away from the front door on the other side of the table. They were grimly silent. A half bottle of gin stood open on the table. Two glasses, still holding enough gin to top-up the bottle at the table, were at its side. There were two other detectives apart from the one with blood-shot eyes and the white one. They were both black.

'Who are these boys?' the white detective asked, addressing the question to Tauyo or Rudo.

But before either could reply, Sam asked the white man:

'Are you a police officer?'

'Watch it, little bastard!' the white man replied angrily.

'If you are a police officer, I would like to see your identification, please.'

Sam spoke very clamly and with his usual deliberateness.

'What do you think you are?' the white man demanded.

'Did you have a search warrant when you came into the house?'

The white man threw a search warrant at Sam:

'Read that if you can read!'

'You won't be treating people in this country like this much longer, officer. Did you advise the lady and the gentleman of their rights before arresting them?'

'Listen, little boy. You don't talk to your elders in that way. Where is your African mentality?'

'I reserve that for my African elders—'

'You cannot talk to a senior officer so rudely, young man!' the detective with blood-shot eyes interjected.

'Shut up! I don't talk to niggers. And you are a nigger!' replied Sam.

The blood-shot eyed detective flew at Sam and started furiously boxing the boy. Rudo screamed and yelled. Tauya pleaded with the policeman to stop boxing Sam. Sam was on the floor. Alexio, fuming with anger, tried to snatch the bottle of gin and smash it on the black detective. But the other two detectives held him. They manhandled Alexio. The white man stood and watched the scene.

The red-eyed detective was about to crush his foot into Alexio's face but Alexio grabbed the foot with both hands.

The black detective fell backwards. Sam was trying to get up when the white detective viciously booted Sam in the eyes. Sam screamed and cursed. The detective whose foot had now been freed, kneed Sam in the stomach and repeatedly knocked Sam's head on the concrete floor. When the white man finally restrained the black detective, Sam had lost consciousness. Blood was oozing out from a gash somewhere at the back of Sam's head.

The white man ordered Rudo and Tauya to be taken out to the car. As soon as Alexio was freed by the two black detectives who held him, he rushed to Sam.

'Sam! Sam! I will go and call an abulance.' Sam could not answer. Alexio dashed out of the house to try and run to Machipisa, half a mile away, to telephone for an ambulance. When he got outside, there was a huge crowd of people. Alexio's hands, clothes and face were covered in Sam's blood. Alexio was sweating and crying. He was moving towards the police car. He wanted to plead with the white man to take Sam to hospital. It would be quicker than calling an ambulance from Harare Hospital, some four miles away.

'Sam is dying there! They won't take him to hospital! My friend is dying there! But they can't take him to hospital!' Alexio repeated as he moved towards the car.

'Don't let that car leave before it takes Sam to hospital! Please! Please!' There was much pain in Alexio's voice.

The crowd was buzzing. People wanted to know what was going on. But nobody really knew. A scuffle broke out between the policemen and Rudo and Tauya. The white man was holding a revolver in his hand. He was shaking. The African detectives were trying to shove Rudo and Tauya into the car, but Rudo and Tauya were resisting. A few people were helping them to resist getting into the car by pulling them back. Alexio finally reached the car. Yelling hysterically, he started scratching and smearing Sam's blood on the face of the blood-shot eyed detective. At that moment, three land-rovers with riot-police and Alsatian dogs arrived. The white detectives in the Austin Westminster shouted at the crowd to disperse. But the crowd which was swelling all the time, did not look as though it was going to disperse. The white detective fired a shot in the air. Not everybody, including the arriving policemen, knew who had fired the shot. People in the crowd responded to this revolver shot by throwing stones, sticks, bottles and anything they could pick up at the police cars. Black police reservists, armed with thick truncheons, rushed out of the land-rovers and began pounding anyone they could reach. The white policemen armed with automatic assault rifles climbed on top of the land-rovers, ready to shoot. Five other white policemen armed with revolvers unleashed the Alsatian dogs on the crowd. People were fleeing and throwing stones as they ran. A number of people were arrested. They were literally being thrown into the land-rovers. After a while, only Alexio, Rudo, Tauya and the policemen were left. Except for Alexio, they all got into their cars and drove away. Alexio stood alone and watched the police cars drive away. Tears were streaming down his face. The cars disappeared, and he walked back into the house.

Alexio knew Sam was dead. But he didn't know for sure. He had never seen a dead person before. He walked to the house next door. He asked the man there how one could tell if a man was dead or not. The man and his wife returned to Rudo's house with Alexio. Sam's body lay in a pool of blood. The woman took one glance at Sam's body and the blood and went out. She began wailing. The man suggested to Alexio that they clean the blood off Sam's body and cover him with a blanket. But the man seemed to lack the courage to do it. Alexio took several rags from Rudo and Tauya's bedroom and cleaned the blood off his dead friend. Now Alexio had stopped crying. Neighbours began arriving at the house. The women wailed. Alexio suggested they carried Sam's body into the spare room. The men carried Sam's body.

Alexio asked one of the men to go and call Mbuya but on a second thought decided he himself should go. He walked out of the house. The sun was going down. Alexio was in a trance. He could see the sun, but he couldn't think what time of the day it was. He didn't feel sure he could remember how to get to Mbuya's house until he got there. He met a group of police reservists patrolling the area. They questioned him about where he was going and where he was coming from. They asked him why he was covered in blood. Alexio explained and they let him go. Tears started streaming down again. He felt all his energy leave him.

When Mbuya saw Alexio, she knew about Sam. She began to wail.

'Where is he, Alexio? Where is your friend, Sam? Where is Sam? Where is my husband?'

She and Alexio embraced. Mbuya was now wailing loudly and Alexio was crying. With their arms round each other Mbuya and Alexio walked back to Rudo's house. People who knew her or Sam or Alexio and neighbours began following behind silently. Mbuya was wailing and saying things about Sam in the manner of a liturgy. At Rudo's house, they went into the room where Sam's body was. On seeing Sam's body, Mbuya completely broke down. Alexio passed out. After an hour, an ambulance arrived and took Sam's body to hospital where a doctor confirmed Sam was dead.

People were sent out to inform Sam's mother and immediate relatives. Party officials and friends came. Rudo and Tauya were refused permission to attend Sam's funeral because they were not 'members of the immediate family'. Sam was mourned for three days before being buried at the Highfields cemetry. A week later, Tauya and Rudo were convicted for illegal possession and consumption of alcoholic spirits and resisting arrest. They were both sentenced to six months imprisonment. The policeman who killed Sam was charged with culpable homicide, found guilty and given a two-year suspended sentence.

Alexio and Mbuya visited both Tauya and Rudo in prison. Rudo pleaded with Mbuya to move into Rudo's house and look after Alexio. For weeks, Alexio did not go to school. He spent most of his time alone brooding or with Mbuya.

'Alexio, you are all I have left. It's hard but you must try and forget Sam. You must go back to school,' Mbuya used to say.

She had resumed going to the market. She tried, as much as she could, to live as before. But she used to make mistakes. She would call Alexio Sam and that opened the wounds again.

Alexio resumed going to school, but now, he was a very subdued boy who only did what he had to do. He didn't want to make any new friends. At the end of that year, he finished his grade eight coming top of his class. When he got home, Mbuya asked him:

'I know you passed, but in what position?'

'I came second.'

'It's very good. I should have expected you to come top but it's understandable. You missed much school. Who came top, then?'

'Oh, another boy.'

'Listen, Alexio. The last time I visited Rudo, we discussed your future. We both think you ought to go to secondary school.'

'Mbuya, where are the fees going to come from? Rudo and Tauya are both in prison. When they come out they will need every penny. It's not going to be easy for them to get any jobs with unemployment as it is.'

'I am coming to that. Rudo spoke with an official of the Party who can help you with fees and clothes for your first two years at secondary school.'

'Mbuya, what's the point of it all? I may get an easy desk job as a clerk but the money won't be that good. I think it's a waste of both money and time.'

'Alexio, whether you like it or not, you are going to secondary school. You hear me?' Mbuya told Alexio very firmly.

On the strength of his grade eight examination performance, Alexio had been offered several places at mission boarding schools and one government boarding school. The place at the government school came with a third of his fees paid. So he accepted the place at the government boarding school just outside Salisbury.

Throughout the three years that Alexio lived in Salisbury every school holiday, he had visited his mother at Mtoko before going down to stay with his uncle, Gomo, at Makosa. At Mtoko, he stayed a few days helping his mother in the fields, and in her vegetable garden. Alexio's mother was an excellent potter. Since Alexio first went to Salisbury, she had begun making pots and other things which she sold. The money, she sent to Rudo to help with the upkeep of Alexio. She held Rudo in high esteem.

At Makosa, Alexio was given much affection and respect, not only by Gomo and the family, but by many of the villagers. People asked him to go to their huts for meals. They would ask him questions about what was happening in the city. They looked up to him to explain many things that were taking place in the country. Alexio imparted to them everything he knew. He spoke to Chief Makosa about the Party and the Chief decided to form a branch of the Party in the village.

Everyone talked about how Alexio had not been changed much by living in the city.

'He is still as respectful and hard-working as he always was. He is our son. The son of the whole village. He has grown from the very soil we till here at Makosa. A real son of the soil,' Chief Makosa used to say.

Chief Makosa always summoned Alexio for an audience a day or so after the boy arrived in the village. They would talk late into the night. The Chief would ask Alexio:

'What shall we do? The government keeps on reducing our cultivating land. They still keep reducing the number of cattle per family. They say it's to make everything better. But you can see for yourself, things are getting worse all the time. We reap less than we used to. They are taking the most fertile land away. Year after year they are increasing taxes. Alexio, things can't go on like this. What can we do?'

After passing her grade five, Joy also went to Salisbury to live with her brother and do grade six. Like Alexio, she went to Makosa during all her school holidays. Both in Salisbury and at Makosa, Joyce and Alexio spent much time together. Now, their relationship was an open love affair. Everybody expected them to marry some day. At Makosa, on some days they both worked at Gomo's fields or Joy's parent's fields. When they were free, they took long walks and talked and picked up wild fruit. In Salisbury, they used to spend much time with Sam and Sam's various girl-friends.

After his grade eight examination, Alexio visited Rudo

and Tauya in their respective prisons. He and Joy travelled as far as Mtoko together. Alexio stopped to see his mother at Mtoko and Joy proceeded to Makosa. When he arrived at Mtoko, Alexio found that his mother wasn't feeling too well. She complained of stomach pains but nobody really knew what the trouble was. Alexio insisted on taking his mother to the mission clinic at Mtoko. She agreed. They went to the clinic and Ma Chiko was admitted for observation. She suggested to her son that he proceed to Makosa but to come back and visit her before going to his new school near Salisbury. Since she wasn't really very ill, Alexio agreed and left for Makosa.

Alexio did not stay long at Makosa. A few days after his arrival there, he got a message that his mother was seriously ill. By the time he arrived at Mtoko, she had died. Tendayi had contracted typhoid in the clinic. Gomo and both his wives came for Tendayi's funeral. Alexio felt very bitter about his mother's death.

He stayed a few weeks at his mother's huts before he left for Salisbury and stayed at Rudo's house. She and Tauya were still in prison.

Alexio had cried when his mother died, but he really had not understood what her death meant to him. The reality of her death took time to penetrate into his hardened emotions. When it did, about six weeks after her death, he broke down. But Mbuya and Joyce were there to see him through it. Alexio recovered from his breakdown in time to go to the secondary school at Goromonzi at the beginning of the first term.

Goromonzi Secondary School was one of the only two government or state schools for Africans that went up to the sixth form. The fees were high but not as high as at mission schools. The school was modelled on the English public school. The headmaster and some of the teachers were white. In fact, most of the teachers were white. It was a mixed school. It offered both science and arts subjects. Getting a place at Goromonzi or Fletcher was a highly competitive business.

When Alexio arrived there, he wasn't sure about his academic ability amongst the best students from various schools. In the first year, he concentrated on his studies. He did very well in both arts and science subjects.

Part of Alexio's fees were being paid for by a Party official in his private capacity. He was a young man, recently married and wanted to help. The name of this man was Marufo.

Marufo, as Alexio's sponsor, received school reports on Alexio's academic performance. He found these very good. Now and again, Marufo and his wife visited Alexio. Alexio wrote to both Marufo and his wife very regularly. During school holidays, Alexio spent some days with Marufo and his family, helping as much as he could. But most of his time he spent at Makosa with his uncle, Gomo.

When Rudo and Tauya came out of prison, they had both changed markedly. They shunned their friends. They stopped going to Party meetings. A few weeks after they were released, they joined a church called The Apostles. They had to give up drinking and smoking and eating pork. Soon, instead of remaining politically non-active, they became actively anti-political. After some time, they succeeded in converting Mbuya to their religion. For a long time Rudo and Tauya could not get jobs. But eventually, through a member of their church, they got jobs. Rudo as a cook and Tauya as a garden boy.

Joy was still in Salisbury doing her grade eight. Students at Goromonzi were allowed to go into Salisbury for the day on Saturdays and occasionally for whole weekends, if they had good reasons. Alexio regularly visited her in Harare. The first time he went to visit Joy in Salisbury, he was given a lift by a white couple who taught him. Their names were Paul and Sarah Davies. She took him for English and he, Latin. They were both in their late twenties. Mr and Mrs Davies drove into Salisbury many times a week. They always used to offer Alexio a lift into town. One day they asked Alexio if he wanted to go into town. He said he didn't have any business in town. They invited him for the ride and he agreed. When they came back from Salisbury that day, Mr and Mrs Davies invited Alexio to their house for supper and he accepted. They talked a lot that evening. Mr and Mrs Davies were British. They had come to Rhodesia to teach under a voluntary scheme. They were in

Rhodesia on a contract for two years. They were finding life in Rhodesia rather frustrating as the laws of the country did not allow them to mix socially with black people as much as they liked to.

'When we came here, we wanted to meet Africans but it's almost impossible. We need passes to visit African townships or reserves. The only place where we can meet Africans are one bar in the city or at the University or as students at school, or as our servants . . .' Mrs Davies had said.

During his second year at Goromonzi, Alexio became close friends with the British couple. This upset the headmaster and other white members of the staff. As a result, the police visited Paul and Sarah Davies and reminded them of some of the laws of the land that governed race relations. In the end the police had no choice but to keep a close watch on their movements.

One sunny April Monday morning, Alexio was having his Art lesson. The headmaster came and asked Alexio to accompany him to the school office. The headmaster did not tell Alexio what he wanted to talk to the boy about. When they walked into the headmaster's office, there were two men: one white and the other black. Alexio thought they looked like detectives. They were. The headmaster introduced them as Detective Superintendent Freeman and Sergeant Bonga.

'We would like you to come to the police station to help us with inquiries we are making in Salisbury,' said Detective Superintendent Freeman.

'What are these inquiries you are making in Salisbury?' Alexio asked.

'We can't discuss that here. I would also like to see your place in your dormitory,' said Freeman.

'Do you have a search warrant?'

'Er—no.'

Alexio did not have anything to hide and although Freeman did not have a search warrant, Alexio thought it best to agree to have his place searched. The headmaster accompanied Alexio and the two Special Branch men to the dormitory where Alexio lived.

The detectives went through all Alexio's mail and took all

letters from Marufo and his wife. They also took Alexio's essays on English literature. They ripped open the mattress and pillow on his bed searching for hidden documents. But they found nothing. After a thorough examination of everything Alexio owned, the detectives led him back to the headmaster's office and drove to Salisbury with him. At the police station, they interrogated Alexio about his friendship with Marufo.

'How do you know Marufo?' asked Freeman.

Alexio explained.

'Why do you know Marufo?'

Alexio said he did not know how to answer such a question.

'Why are you interested in politics?'

The boy said he wasn't. Freeman read one letter that Alexio had written to Marufo. It was now in Freeman's hands because the police had searched Marufo's house in Highfields. According to Freeman the letter was subversive and contravened the Preservation of Constitutional Government Act. Freeman had no choice but to charge Alexio.

Alexio asked to be allowed to read the letter. Freeman gave it to him. After reading it, Alexio said:

'I don't see how this letter could contravene the Act since it was written to a private individual.'

Freeman told Alexio he was talking a lot of bullshit.

Freeman would go ahead and charge him.

'I am sorry sir, but you can't charge me,' said the boy with much satisfaction.

'Why not? You will see my boy.'

'This letter is dated 28 March and the Preservation of Constitution Bill became an Act on the 29th of March.'

Freeman was rather short and stocky. He had a thick moustache, and a hard face. His eyes were large and somewhat kind. Freeman, his eyes rolling like someone having a fit, snatched up the letter from the table. Alexio was right; he could not be charged. Freeman stood up and punched the boy on the jaw.

'You are very clever. But not so clever!'

Freeman went out of the small room where the interrogation was being conducted. A short time later,

Freeman came back. In quite a friendly voice he asked Alexio:

'Why do you go to school?'

'To be educated, sir.'

'And what do you want to do when you are educated?'

'To help my people, sir.'

'And also to make money.'

'Yes, sir.'

'Let me tell you this, my boy. Money is the greatest thing in the world. Some of us admit it but others don't. But we all want to make money. Don't you think that's right?'

'I can't say, sir.'

'Alexio, you are an intelligent boy. You could make yourself a lot of money if you wanted to. You will never need to worry about your school fees or clothes again . . . I want you to help me—me personally and not the police. Do you want to help me?'

'Of course, sir. If I can.'

'All I want is for us to keep in touch. If you hear anything at school or from Marufo, you telephone me. I will give you my telephone number before you go. I will give you thirty pounds a month. This arrangement is just between you and me. Are we agreed?' said Freeman, extending his hand to shake Alexio's. The boy did not take it.

'Sir, I am a citizen of this country. If I see anyone committing an offence, I think it is my duty to report them to the police. Why should I be paid for doing my duty?'

'Alexio, don't be foolish. You know very well what I am talking about. If you want more money, of course we can talk about it.'

'I don't want any money, sir. But I can promise you that if I see someone killing another person, the first thing I shall think of is going to the police.'

'If you want to be too clever, that's not my problem. Think about your education and your future. I am going to keep an eye on you. That's for sure. And sooner or later, I will get you.'

Freeman questioned Alexio about Joy and the teachers, Paul and Sarah Davies. Finally, Freeman said to Alexio:

'Marufo is in prison. We arrested him last night. We are going to make sure he remains there for a long time. If I were you I would start thinking about where I am going to get my next term's school fees. All right, you will be driven back to your school.'

Alexio was driven to school. To solve the problem once and for all, Alexio told anybody who cared to ask that the police were trying to make him an informer. By the end of that day, almost everyone in the school knew about this.

Two days later Freeman came again and took Alexio into Salisbury. In fact, these visits were to be as regular as four times a week for the next three months. Freeman came at night, in the early hours of the morning—anytime he chose. At the end of that term, Alexio almost failed his examinations. That school holiday, Alexio decided to stay in Salisbury. Freeman had demanded to know all Alexio's movements over the holiday period. Alexio did not want to stay at Rudo and Tauya's because of their attitude towards politics. Marufo and his wife were both in prison. So he was glad to accept when a school friend offered him accommodation in a house in Mufakose Township, eight miles west of Salisbury. After a few days, the school friend and his family left for their village leaving Alexio alone in their house.

One day Alexio and Joy, who had not yet left for Makosa, discussed Alexio's troubles. They concluded that, if Alexio was to continue with his education, he would have to leave the country. They contacted Paul and Sarah for advice. Paul offered to help. Immediately he wrote to his father in England asking him if he could give Alexio accommodation and find him a place to study. In the meantime, Alexio made an application for a passport.

When Alexio submitted his application for a passport, he had been told to return a week later. Joy decided to go to Makosa for about four days.

A week later was a Thursday. Alexio's plans for the day were quite straight forward. He woke up early and prepared to go into town. He had to go and see about his passport. He was to meet Paul and Sarah outside the passport office. Then they would go into the passport office to see if his passport was ready.

After the passport business, he, Paul and Sarah would probably go to the University—one of the few places they could eat together, for lunch. Alexio knew Joy was arriving in Salisbury from Makosa early that evening. He would visit her at her brother's house in Harare township in the evening. If he could, he would stay at her brother's house; otherwise he would catch the last bus back to Mufakose. Thus, his mind clear about how he was going to spend the day, he walked out of the house to the bus terminal and caught the bus into the city.

BOOK THREE: CLOSING A CIRCLE

AT ELEVEN O'CLOCK, it was already hot as Alexio got off the bus at Railway Avenue terminal, next to the Central Investigation Department headquarters. Slowly, he began walking towards the passport office under a merciless August sun. The passport office was on the corner of Second Street and Jamieson Avenue. Alexio decided to go to the longer but simpler way. He walked eastwards up Railway Avenue until he came to Second Street where he turned left. Knowing he would not be meeting Paul and Sarah much before noon, he lazily strolled down Second Street. He stopped, took off his light navy blue blazer and carried it over his shoulder before continuing his slow walk. Even walking so slowly did not help. By the time he got to Cecil Square, beads of sweat had formed on his forehead and were beginning to condense into streams of sweat. He was walking along the side of the Square. He looked around for a bench but most of them were occupied—mainly by elderly white people. As he came level with the water-fountain, he spotted an unoccupied bench under a jacaranda tree. He went over and sat down. Alexio was facing Salisbury Cathedral. He wiped the sweat off his face and neck before lighting a cigarette. Blankly, he gazed out in the direction of the Cathedral. Then he noticed white people coming out of the Cathedral. Yes, even on such a hot Thursday morning, a wedding was taking place. Something unclear, something connected with the wedding, made him start thinking about Joy. He always kept a photograph of her in his small black plastic wallet. He took it out from the inside pocket of his blazer and looked at the photograph for some time. A smile formed on his face and then he put his wallet back into the pocket. Now he felt a weak breeze flow into his body through his open-necked shirt. It was best to move on while the breeze was still blowing. He walked back into Second Street past a few more benches occupied by white people. Many white people lay scattered all over the Square. Alexio continued his walk along Second Street.

Very soon the breeze died down. The air became very still again. A smell of car exhaust fumes hit Alexio's nostrils. It was only then that he became conscious of the noise of the cars, lorries, delivery vans and buses rolling past in both directions. When he came to the entrance of the passport office, he saw a group of black people standing in the doorway and thought them stupid for blocking the entrance. But as he tried to enter, he realized they were in a double queue. He glanced at the white section and saw only four people. A big lorry drove past making much noise. Alexio felt very irritated: 'I am going to be here all day' he thought as he stood leaning against the wall of the passport office and breathing in the exhaust fumes. He wondered why he shouldn't go to Mtoko.

Standing there, he felt hungry, mildly dizzy and slightly nervous. He knew he could not stand in the queue until his turn. But he had to wait for Paul and Sarah anyway; so he couldn't leave.

Both Paul and Sarah had a habit of not starting conversations from the beginning. They always began as if they were continuing from some point the last conversation left off. They arrived on foot a little earlier than twelve o'clock. Alexio had expected them in their old Zephyr-six.

'Afternoon,' said Alexio weakly.

'You are not going to make us spend the whole day here, are you?' Sarah greeted Alexio, as she looked at the queue.

'You look as if you are going to pass out any minute. What's wrong?' Paul asked.

'Are you ill?' asked Sarah. Alexio was still trying to muster enough strength to answer the first question.

That was another thing about Paul and Sarah. They never waited for replies.

'I am hot, tired, hungry and annoyed.'

'That solves the problem! Let's go to the University and have lunch,' suggested Sarah enthusiastically. It had been obvious since they arrived that she did not want to wait in the long queue. But she had not been sure how Alexio would feel about leaving the passport business till later.

'Don't be so bloody daft, Sarah. We have just left the car at the garage,' said Paul.

'We can catch a bus, Genius!' replied Sarah, playfully hitting her husband.

'With Alexio?! Sarah, at times you amaze me.'

They could not catch a bus to the University together

because the buses which served that area were for white people only.

'How about a picnic lunch in Salisbury Park?' Alexio suggested.

'Right. Let's go somewhere and get drinks and sandwiches,' agreed Paul.

'Let's move then. I am dying of hunger,' said Alexio trying to look and sound worse than he really felt.

'Are you sure you don't mind leaving this passport business until later?' asked Paul.

'Yes, I mind. I mind very much,' said Alexio as he led the way to cross Second Street.

The traffic lights were amber before they were to turn to red to stop Second Street traffic and enable them to cross. Someone placed a hand on Alexio's shoulder. Alexio turned to see who it was. It was neither Paul nor Sarah.

'There is a document you are required to sign in there', said a white man, half whispering and pointing to the passport office. By the time Alexio turned round to face the speaker, the man was already walking towards the passport office. Momentarily, Alexio felt an intense attack of nerves. But just as quickly, he recovered. He looked at the white man, but all he could see now was a large behind of a short fat man dressed in a white short-sleeved shirt, grey flannel trousers and sandals. At the entrance to the passport building, the white man turned round to see if Alexio was following. Alexio was still standing wondering if the man had made a mistake. The white man beckoned. Alexio started walking back to the passport office and the man disappeared inside.

'What did he say, Alexio?' Paul asked. Alexio did not answer. His mind was racing over everything. An attack of nerves always told him something was wrong. What could it be? Within the time it took to walk the few yards between the traffic lights and the passport office, he tried to think of anything that might have been wrong with his passport application forms. He could think of nothing. He entered the passport office. Paul and Sarah were close behind him.

The white man was now behind a counter. He yelled at the people in the queue to make way. Most of the black people looked at Alexio. Their faces seemed to be saying: 'Who are you to be jumping the queue like this?! A sell-out! An informer!' But they made way for him. Alexio noticed two white men in the African queue. They were looking at him too. Maybe they were here to get passports for their servants, Alexio thought.

When he reached the counter, the man bent down behind the counter. He fumbled with some papers before standing upright again. Addressing Alexio, he asked:

'What did you say your name was again?'

'I didn't say,' replied Alexio.

'What is your name, boy?' asked the white man who had a puffy face and very small blue eyes that were buried in swollen eyelids. Alexio wanted to know what was wrong. He decided he would not know any quicker by asking the white man why he thought it was Alexio who was required to sign the documents since the white man did not know Alexio's name. Instead, he stated:

'Alexio Shonga'

'Alexio what?'

'Alexio Shonga!' Alexio did not now feel nervous, or hungry or tired.

For a few long moments, the white man seemed to stare through Alexio before he bent down again. Then:

'You are Alexio Shonga?' asked someone from behind. Alexio turned round. It was one of the two white men in the African queue.

'That's correct,' Alexio replied wondering what was going on.

'I am Detective Sergeant Wright from Special Branch, Railway Avenue. We have a few questions we would like to ask you. You will accompany me to the police station.'

'What is it in connection with?' Alexio asked.

'You will find out when we get there.'

Wright was lean and tall. He had intensely blue eyes and closely cropped golden hair. He could have been a handsome man but for his aquiline nose and severe face.

Paul and Sarah moved closer to Alexio and Wright. Paul asked what was going on. Alexio replied that he didn't know.

'What is all this in connection with, Officer?' Paul addressed Wright.

'You are Mr and Mrs Davies?'

Paul and Sarah said they were.

'We would like you also to accompany us to the police station to answer a few questions.'

'We have a right to know what this is all about. Unless we know, we are not coming!' shouted Sarah.

Wright ignored her. He and another white man, a detective named Steer, sandwiched Alexio between them and started walking out of the passport office. Perhaps it was all in Alexio's head, but the black faces in the queue seemed to have changed; 'I commiserate, I commiserate,' each face seemed to be saying now. Paul and Sarah were following.

Wright led the party to a two-door Ford Anglia parked on Second Street. Alexio discovered that the party included a black man—an assistant detective called John.

As the car sped off towards Railway Avenue, Paul asked again:

'Could you please tell us what all this is about?'

'Ask your friend, Mr Shonga, here. If you are such good friends, he ought to have told you a long time ago. He knows everything,' said Wright.

'Alexio, what do you know about this?' asked Paul.

Alexio replied; 'I know nothing at all'. He didn't sound convincing. Paul gave up. Wright had scored a point.

The CID Headquarters in Railway Avenue was a dull, cream painted old colonial building. Wright drove to the back of the building into a big car park. They all got out of the car and entered the building through a rear entrance. Wright led them up a flight of stairs to the second floor. Inside the building it was much cooler and the air smelt of dampness. They came to some double steel gates. The gates were guarded by four black men armed with truncheons.

'John, take care of Shonga until I call,' said Wright, 'Mr and Mrs Davies, this way please.' Paul and Sarah were led by Wright and Steer to an office on the right side of a long and not very wide corridor. They were taken into a reception room for whites. Wright left them there with Steer. He walked up to the third floor and knocked on a door before he entered.

'Any luck?' asked a medium-sized, middle aged man who was sitting behind a large desk. His name was Bradshaw. He had attractive features and silvery grey hair.

'Yes sir. They are all downstairs.'

'Any problems?'

Bradshaw had a very English accent. In fact, he had only recently arrived from England. He had worked for Scotland Yard for the previous eleven years. He had left Scotland Yard for a higher post in Rhodesia. It offered better pay and better working conditions.

'No sir,' replied Wright, 'But they nearly gave us the slip. I think they had smelt a rat and decided to get away.'

'Paul and Sarah Davies? Do I have their files up here?'

'No sir.'

'Get the files and bring the two in. You work on this boy, Alexander or whatever his name is.'

'Name of Shonga, sir. Alexio Shonga.'

'Yes, Alexio . . . Er, Wright?'

'Sir'

'I want you to try this one on the boy. It's an old one from the Germans. Before you start the interrogation give him a reception.'

'Reception, sir?'

'Invite everyone into your office. As many people as you can get into the little room. Once you get him in there, make as much noise as possible. About him. But I don't want any violence. In fact, avoid any physical violence. Keep it up for a minute or two. Have him in the centre. Don't invite any coloured officers. I want a report on the effect afterwards.'

'No Africans, sir?'

'You know what I mean, Wright,' said Bradshaw, who still called blacks coloureds, as people in England did.

Wright went down to the second floor and got a thick file on which was written in bold red ink: DAVIES, P. & S. He walked to the white reception room and went in. He asked Paul and Sarah to follow him up. They went to Bradshaw's office.

Inside Bradshaw's office, Paul and Sarah sat on chairs facing him.

'Now what's the trouble?' beamed Bradshaw somewhat cheerfully, considering Paul and Sarah's circumstances.

'You should ask!' sneered Sarah.

'There is no need for that Mrs Davies. All I want is a friendly chat with you. You young people come out to a beautiful country like this where you should enjoy life to the full, but you don't. Er, I must tell you right away that you are *not* under arrest or anything like that. A few reports about you being mixed up with local politics have been coming in a little too often. Like you, I am British. From Hove in Sussex. Worked for Scotland Yard in London for eleven years. Where are you two from, Mrs Davies?'

'Paul is a Londoner. I am from Coventry.'

'My younger brother lives in Coventry. We spent a month with him and his family just before we came out.'

'How long have you been out here?' asked Paul.

'Barely seven months. Yes. Seven months. And where did you two meet?' asked Bradshaw with fatherly warmth.

'Isn't it all in the file?' said Sarah caustically.

'Leeds, we both went to Leeds,' said Paul.

'I sent my boy to Newcastle. The girl went to Sussex. It was nearer home. They are both married now and settled in London, thank God. You young people these days! You think you know everything. You have this new craze of left-wing politics at the universities. Oh! I don't know . . . Turning to this thing. The people here—I mean the whites, have a terrible hate for communism. They are not as open-minded about politics as people are in England. They have a real fear here. Those who accept left-wing politics are worried about the—about the—er, Africans—the blacks, because they fear the blacks will take these things seriously. I mean in England, who would care what anyone said at Hyde Park? But here, the situation is different . . . The only thing I really want to know from you is where this coloured boy, your friend, is going to?'

'Mr Bradshaw, Alexio is a very bright boy. My mother has just agreed to look after him while he goes to the Polytechnic to do his 'A' Levels. There is no question he will make university—' replied Paul.

'I know all that, I know all that. Why can't he study here in his own country?'

'We teach at his school. The police come for him three or four times a week. At all sorts of times of the day. And do you know why they harass him like that? Because of his friendship with a nationalist politician! The man used to pay Alexio's fees. Seriously Mr Bradshaw, you don't really believe a boy like that is dangerous to this facist government?! It makes me puke!' said Paul.

'Now, Davies. Let's not be emotional. Let me ask you this. You do want to help this boy, don't you?'

'We are not sending him to any communist country. We—'

'If you want to help him, you are not going about it the right way. You want to tone down a bit. You know, the worst that could happen to the two of you is to be deported. But your friend could end up in prison, detention camp or a restriction camp. Now that would not be helping him, would it? As I have said, try to tone down a bit.'

'Why have you arrested him?' asked Sarah.

'He is not arrested. He is here just to answer a few questions. Don't worry about him. I can assure you he will be released. I trust what you have told me is true. You don't know the number of these people who leave the country in the name of going abroad to study and end up in communist guerilla training camps. If we don't check these things now we could find ourselves with a big problem in a few year's time. Any way that is that.'

Bradshaw offered Paul and Sarah some tea. They sat and talked about England. Finally Bradshaw rang Wright and asked him if he was through with Alexio. Not yet. He wouldn't be for some time. Bradshaw accompanied Paul and Sarah down to the second floor and told them they could wait for Alexio if they wished to. Bradshaw had to go out to lunch. Paul and Sarah thanked him and said goodbye.

Meanwhile John had taken Alexio into a small waiting room which was immediately beyond the steel-gates. The floor of the room was littered with cigarette ash and stubs. The air was stale with the smell of tobacco. A rough and continuous bench ran along three walls of the room. There was a small barred window on the far side, away from the door. John had shoved Alexio into the room and yelled at him, to sit down. Alexio sat facing the doorway with the window behind him.

'What have you been up to?' John asked Alexio.

'When?' asked Alexio.

'*When*? Why are you here?'

'I don't know.'

'Yeah! That's what you all say when you first come in. There is no hurry, my boy. You are going to tell us everything.'

Alexio thought it was best to avoid arguing. He knew he could end up being beaten even before interrogation.

'Would you like a cigarette?' he asked offering John one. John looked at him and took one. John lit the cigarettes. At that point two other African detectives walked in with a man. At the doorway, one of the two detectives, David, placed his hands on the shoulders of the man and violently pushed him into the waiting room. The man stumbled in and crashed into John. The man fell down. John 'welcomed' him with a hard kick on the face while the man was still on the dirty floor.

'He is very eager to come in here, isn't he?' said John. The detectives laughed. Alexio was looking at the man all the time.

'Where did you pick up this one?' asked John pointing to the man as if he was a thing.

'At the Hostels in Harare,' David answered.

'And what has he been up to?'

'He is right here. Help yourself.'

John poked his shoe into the man's face and said:

'Come on! Get up! What have you been up to at the Hostels then?'

The man staggered up. He was bleeding from the mouth and from the nose. By appearance, the man could have been in his early fifties. All he wore was a tattered short-sleeved khaki shirt and short khaki trousers which were relatively new. He wiped the blood off his nose with his bare hand and rubbed the hand on the back of his trousers and shirt.

'I have asked you a question!' shouted John shaking his fist in the man's face.

'They say I was singing a political song in the shower at the

Hostel last night.'

'And you are going to tell me that you were not?'

'I *know*. I was not singing—'

'Then why do they say it was you?'

'That's what I can't understand.'

'So you think they are stupid enough to say that you were doing something you were not doing, eh?'

'No. I don't say that, I—'

'Then what do you say?'

'The police are quite right, somebody was whistling a political tune when people were taking showers last night. I heard it myself. But I don't know who it was.'

'And yours, John?' asked David.

'Now, don't mess around with this one. Wright's job. Besides, one day this boy might become my brother-in-law. Can you imagine what a beauty his sister could be?'

Saying that seemed to give John an idea. He walked over to Alexio and told him to empty all his pockets. Alexio did. The wallet, some letters he had received, some letters he was going to post, an address book and some coins. John started by going through the address book but it did not interest him much. He looked in the wallet and his attention was caught by Joy's photograph.

'Hey! Come and see!' he called the other two detectives, 'What did I tell you!'

'How do you know it's not his girl friend?' asked David's partner.

'Because *he* told me it's his sister. She is there, man! Isn't she your sister?' John asked Alexio.

'Sure.'

'What's sure?' asked David glaring at Alexio.

'That she is my sister.'

'I told you. She is his sister!'

Wright appeared in the doorway. All of a sudden the bullying African detectives were like little boys who had been caught doing something naughty.

'Alexio!' Wright called and beckoned the African boy to follow. Alexio picked up his address book, wallet, letters and the coins and put them in the pocket of his jacket. John handed him back Joy's picture. Wright, with both hands in his pockets, was now some way down the long corridor. He was whistling a tune. John trotted past Alexio and asked Wright if he would be needed. Wright rudely told him he wasn't needed. John walked back to the waiting room, and gave Alexio a sympathetic look as they passed each other. Wright now stood before the doorway of a room on the left. When Alexio was near Wright, Wright made an exaggerated theatrical gesture for Alexio to enter the room. Alexio walked to the doorway. Abruptly, he stopped and looked questioningly at Wright.

'Come on, Mr Shonga,' he said sarcastically and started edging Alexio into the room. The room was packed with men. White men. Although the door was open, Alexio had not heard their voices until he appeared in the doorway. His heart-beat quickened. It was pounding as if it was trying to leap out of his chest. He felt hot. Very hot. He felt weak in the knees. As Wright edged the boy in, the white men were all very angrily shouting abusive and obscene words at him. The door closed behind him.

'Filthy little nigger!' 'You won't be fucking Sarah, the filthy bitch for a long time, black bastard!' 'Fucking communist!' 'You thought you were clever, eh!' 'When are you going to Moscow then?' 'Tell us—' 'Stupid little nigger!' 'Does Paul watch when you fuck the bitch!' 'You don't know how many problems you've caused us!'

On and on it went. It was difficult for Alexio to hear the rest. Then the climax came. Several of the white men grabbed him and shook him back and forth and from side to side. Wright moved forward and spread his arms around Alexio.

'Come on! Leave him alone!' Wright shouted and pretended to protect Alexio.

Alexio was very scared. It showed. They all saw it on his long brown face. He knew it because of how he felt. Then the door opened and the din suddenly died down. All the white men headed for the door. Like a Sunday School choir, they all filed out of the room. Wright was the last white man to leave the room. Before he went out, he gave an order to Alexio:

'Pick up all that rubbish and put it back in the waste-paper basket,' he said pointing to an overturned waste-paper basket.

'No. I am not yet a prisoner,' replied Alexio calmly. Wright was taken aback by Alexio's reply. Alexio himself was not sure whether he had said what he had said or whether he was simply thinking it.

'It doesn't pay to be clever, my boy. If I were you, I would do what I was told,' said Wright and went out of the room. Alexio wondered whether to pick up the rubbish or not; and decided not to. He started looking around the room. He had heard the door click behind him. It was open. In front of him he could see the buildings outside through two wide windows. That wall was bare but for a big calendar hanging on the wall between the windows. The walls to his right and to the left were covered by blown up photographs. The photographs summed up Wright's career in the British South African Police. Most of them showed Wright in action. Wright: Unleashing an Alsatian on a group of African children. Wright: Sitting on top of a police land-rover with a Thompson sub-machine gun patrolling in an African township. Wright: With a raised truncheon chasing a black woman. The man again: Definitely at Cyril Jennings hall in Highfields, taking notes and tape-recordings at an African public meeting. Wright: Surrounded by a group of African police reservists. Alexio was absorbed in looking at these photographs when someone walked in. It was Steer. Under his arm he had a file and was smoking a cigarette. Steer was as handsome as a bull-dog. When he had first spoken, Alexio had known right away that Steer was a Boer. He spoke in an accented squeaky voice.

'Ekay, I weant to take a statement from you. Simple questions and simple answers, ekay?'

'Yes'

'YES, SIR.'

'Yes, sir,' repeated Alexio.

'And no lies, ekay?'

'No, sir'

Steer sat at the typewriter and went through routine questions. Name. Surname. Date and place of birth, and so forth.

'Noew, you wait for Boss Wright, ekay?'

Steer went out and Alexio was left alone again. He wondered about Paul and Sarah. What was happening to them? He still had not found out why he was there. So they really thought he was sleeping with Sarah! Alexio felt hungry. He thought if he did not eat something soon he was going to faint. He was just wondering if sitting down on one of the chairs would get him in to more trouble when Wright came in.

'Did someone come in and take your particulars?'

'Yes, sir.'

'All right. Come and stand in front of me,' said Wright as he sat behind the desk facing the door.

'When are you leaving for Moscow?' began the interrogation.

'Moscow?'

'Yes! Moscow!'

'Well, I don't know that I am supposed to be going to Moscow.'

'Stop wasting my time. I don't want to hear your lies. We know everything; so the sooner you begin telling the truth the better. Do you understand? You are in trouble, my friend. When are you going to Moscow? The date!'

Alexio took a deep breath.

'I am telling you the honest truth. I don't know anything about going to Moscow.'

Wright gave Alexio a hard despising look.

'I know and you know you are going to Moscow. I will prove it to you. I am going to prove that you know it and you are going to regret that I have had to tell it to you.' Wright opened the file Steer had left and took out a letter and read it to Alexio. It simply began:

Dear Sir,

   This is to inform you that we have received a pre-paid ticket for you to Moscow via London. You may make your reservation any time by either calling at or telephoning our offices. We would be grateful if you could acknowledge receipt of this letter.

                              Yours faithfully,
                              General Manager, CAA

'There. Now are you going to tell me you never saw this letter!'

'No—'

'So you received it then!'

'No, sir'

'Liar! If you tell me one more lie, I will send for "treatment". Do you know what that is?'

'No, sir.'

'Believe me, you don't want to know. You will wish you had never been born.'

'Excuse me, sir, to which address was this letter sent to me?' asked a baffled Alexio.

'That's what I want you to tell me! You are not here to ask me questions! Are you going to tell me everything or not?'

Alexio took another deep breath and sighed:

'I want to tell you everything.'

'Good! Very good. You can start now.'

'Really I know nothing—'

'You are the most terrible liar I have ever come across, Alexio. You mean to tell me you can't tell the truth even once in your life? . . . Why are you applying for a passport?'

'Because I want to go and study in England.'

'I have heard that story from so many of you people. What's wrong with your present school? Why do you want to leave?'

'The police are always visiting me. I can't con- . . .'

'I am not surprised. You are a trouble-maker and look what a mess you have put yourself in now. Does a clever man behave like that? Does he? Come on! Answer me!'

'No, sir.'

'So you see, you are not as clever as you think . . . Do you sleep with Sarah—Mrs Davies?'

'No, sir'

'Do you know what a chronic liar is?'

'Yes, sir'

'That is what you are, Alexio. A chronic liar. We have pictures of you sleeping with her.'

'That is not possible, sir.'

'Are you telling me you would not like to sleep with a white woman? Can you honestly tell me if a white woman asked you to sleep with her you would refuse?'

'Really, sir, I have never thought about it.'

'You are a filthy liar! . . . Are you a member of the African Party?'

'It's banned sir, and it is an offence—'

'You think I don't know that? Were you a member before it was banned?'

'Yes, sir.'

'What do you know about politics? Why did you join it?'

Alexio didn't answer. Had he ever applied for or been offered a scholarship by the Party? Yes, he had applied. When? Three years previously. Well, his scholarship had come through. All Wright wanted to know was Alexio's departure date and the names of the individuals who were organizing 'the scholarship programme'. As he had said before, Alexio really knew nothing about this scholarship or going to Moscow. Then why the hell was he applying for a passport? To go to England. Ah! That was a cheap story to fool the Government. Wright decided to tell Alexio about Alexio's real story. Alexio was a communist, which also explained why he was mixed up with communists like Paul and Sarah Davies. All Alexio wanted to do was to go to Russia 'to become a communist', to receive military training and then to come back to Rhodesia and kill innocent people. Alexio knew that the Government did not like communists. So he was trying to fool the Government by saying he was going to England to study. Did Alexio know that Wright was not a fool either? Alexio was a bloody coward! A stupid idiot! Wasn't that the correct story? No. It wasn't. What Alexio had to understand was that he had not yet committed any criminal offence by being *recruited* for military training as he had not actually trained. Thanks to the intelligence of the police, he would not go for any training. They had saved him from real trouble. Alexio ought to be grateful to them. Now, all Wright wanted was for Alexio to write a statement saying everything Wright had said was true and sign it. After that Wright would let him go. Alexio could not do that. Yes! Yes, he would if he wanted to go home. By the way, his friends, Paul and Sarah were waiting for him outside. The sooner he wrote out this statement, and signed it, the sooner he could go home. It was one-thirty. Wright had to go to lunch. John would bring Alexio some food—what did he like to drink? Milk. There was some paper and a pen. Alexio was going to write the statement over his lunch. He could sit down. Wright walked out.

Alexio was so hungry and felt very weak. He felt so fatigued, he started shaking. He sat on one of the chairs and thought about nothing but food. Years later, John walked in with a small packet of chips and a bottle of milk. John was saying something to Alexio, but the boy hardly heard him as he devoured the chips. When he had finished eating, he drank the milk and lit a cigarette. He wanted to think about what was happening, but he felt so good after eating that for a time everything seemed very remote.

'Give me her address. Please. I will help you get out of this trouble if you do. I can promise you that.' John was saying.

'Whose address?'

'Your sister's. Come on. Please.'

'You don't even know her.'

'Yeah, but I want to know her. What's her name?'

Alexio sensually smoked his cigarette and thought for a few moments. Then he asked:

'The white man and the white woman we came with—Are they still outside?'

'Yes,' replied John.

'Can I talk to them?'

'I can't let you do that. It's not allowed.'

'You want the name and address of my sister?'

'How will I know you are not going to give me a false name and address?'

'Why should I do that? If you don't believe me, why are you asking at all?'

'I can't let you talk to them. I will be in trouble with Mr Wright.'

'You can accompany me to the toilet and I will leave you there for a short time. And if Wright comes back and finds me with my friends you can always say—'

'All right. Give me her name and address.'

'No, only the name now, and the address afterwards.'

'What's her name?'

'Joyce.'

'How can I verify that? Do you have her name in your address book? Show me.'

'Alexio took out Joy's photograph and showed John the back side. Joyce had autographed the picture when she gave it to Alexio.

'Give me the address.'

'I said afterwards.'

'In that case I can't let you speak to them.'

'I will give it to you afterwards.'

'All right. Follow me,' said John, and they walked out of the room.

Paul looked thoroughly bored. Sarah was not there. Paul saw Alexio and stood up.

'Poor bastard! I thought they were never going to let you go!' said Paul thinking Alexio was free to go.

'I am on my way to the toilet. They haven't let me off. I don't think they will.'

'We know they will. Bradshaw assured us.'

'Who is Bradshaw?'

'I think he is the Commissioner. He is British.' Paul made being British sound as though it was the greatest thing in the world.

'What are they asking you about?'

'Everything from being a communist to whether I sleep with Sarah.'

Paul laughed a hearty laugh.

John told Alexio to move on.

'Listen Alexio, there is nothing to worry about. If they don't let you out by four-thirty, I'll get a lawyer. See you later.'

When Alexio and John came back from the toilet, Paul had gone out.

'Don't believe what he told you. Mr Wright can refuse to let you see a lawyer,' said John as they walked back to the room. Wright walked through the steel gates and saw Alexio and John ahead of him in the corridor.

'John! Where are you coming from?'

'Toilet, Boss,' replied John. He stopped before turning round and walking back towards the waiting room.

Alexio walked in to Wright's office and sat down. Wright walked in, carrying his coat over his shoulder.

'Where is it?' demanded Wright.

'Where is what, sir?'

'The statement.'

'There is no statement, sir.'

'THERE IS NO STATEMENT? eh? My boy, you don't realize what a mess you are in. You are swimming hot shit and you are telling me there is no statement! You don't realize! You just don't realize!'

Suddenly, Wright gave Alexio a hard double clap on the ears. Alexio automatically yelled a curse. He was not cursing Wright. He was just cursing. That made Wright go really wild. He tried to box Alexio, but Alexio kept on dodging round the room. Like a frustrated child, Wright leaned out of the door and yelled for John.

John panted into the room.

'Take him downstairs and work on him until he is ready to write and sign a statement! John, I want a proper job! Understand?'

'You will see, Boss.'

John deliberately walked up to Alexio and ordered him to follow. Alexio started following John. But, again very suddenly, John turned round and gave Alexio a great slap on the cheek. The slap floored Alexio. John swung his foot as if he was going to kick Alexio in the face. But he didn't kick him. Instead he kept his foot a few inches from Alexio's face until Alexio, who had covered his face to protect himself, took the hands off his face. John nudged Alexio in the face with his foot. He gripped Alexio's arm and dragged him up and out of the room.

'John?' Wright called again.

'Yes, Boss?'

'Has he been searched?'

'No, Boss.'

'Bring him back, and search him,' said Wright, 'and leave him alone to write the statement when you have finished searching him,' Wright went out.

'Listen small boy, you must not play with Mr Wright. He is a big man here. Tell him what he wants to know. He had a man beaten to death downstairs only two weeks ago . . . Hey, I'm sorry I hit you but I am supposed to do that. I can't refuse, you see. How about the address?'

Alexio refused to give John the address. John thought he would find it in the address book but Alexio did not have it written in that address book. He knew Joy's addresses both at Makosa and in Harare so well that he didn't need to have them written down anyway.

'I must write the statement,' said Alexio to John.

'I know if you write the statement, you will be released today. I shall wait for you at the bus stop and drive you home. I want to meet your sister.'

'OK,' said Alexio and sat down to write. As soon as John walked out, Alexio threw the pen down and lit another cigarette. He felt his swollen face with his hand. He was waiting for Wright. It was a long wait. About an hour and a half later, Wright walked into the room.

'Have you written the statement?'

'No, sir.'

'It doesn't matter now. There has been a terrible mistake . . . you are not the boy we are after. I am sorry. Put your things in your pockets and go. Your friends are waiting outside. I will see you through the gates.'

Alexio and Wright walked along the corridor.

'Have you had your photographs and fingerprints taken?'

'No, sir.'

'Oh,' said Wright looking at his watch, 'it's too late now. Anybody who comes in for questioning has to have photographs and finger-prints taken for the records. I want you to be here at eight-thirty tomorrow morning. Eight-thirty sharp! Do you understand?'

'Yes, sir.'

'If you don't come or you come late, you'll be in real trouble. All right you can go,' said Wright waving Alexio out.

When Alexio walked out of the building, the sun was just setting. Outside, he looked around for Paul and Sarah but could not see them anywhere. He felt very tired. He wondered whether to go and see Joy or to simply go home and think. He had to think about going to the police station the next day. He was worried about it. He made up his mind that if he went to see Joy, she might get worried too. It was best to see her after leaving the police station the following day. He decided to go to Mufakose and started walking towards the bus terminal As he was walking, someone from behind him placed a hand on his shoulder. Alexio was startled! He turned round and saw Paul.

'You must be very tired.'

'I have to be back there tomorrow at eight-thirty in the morning.'

'What for?'

'Fingerprints and photographs, so Wright said. But I don't trust that will be all.'

'Oh, come on. It must be true otherwise he wouldn't have let you out tonight. Let's go and have supper at a friend's house—John. You know John the English bloke. We want to hear what happened today.'

'Paul, I am very tired. All I want is to go home and sleep.'

'Are you sure you don't want to come for supper? We can drop you off in Mufakose afterwards.'

'No. Let me go home.'

Alexio caught the bus to Mufakose.

The next morning, Alexio arrived at the CID headquarters at eight o'clock. He waited in the room where he had waited the previous day. Wright either did not arrive or decided not to attend to Alexio until ten o'clock.

Wright, Freeman, Bonga, and John, Wright's assistant, came into the waiting-room.

'We are going to Mufakose with you so that you can pick up as many clothes as you will need for the next three years. The Minister of Law and Order has ordered that you be sent to a restriction camp for three years. You are a trouble-maker. A political agitator and a communist. We shall do the paper-work when we get back here,' said Wright.

Alexio did not say a word. He regretted having come to the CID headquarters. He should have just disappeared as he had thought the previous evening.

The four detectives and Alexio walked downstairs to the car park. They got into a white Austin Westminster and drove off to Mufakose. Freeman, who was driving, and Wright sitting in the front passenger seat, talked about their friends and families as the car sped to Mufakose. When Freeman tried to ask Alexio the directions, Wright told him not to worry as he knew the way. At the house, Alexio unlocked the door and let them all in. About an hour later, the Special Branch men had a box-full of letters, photographs, notes, newspaper cuttings and various other documents from the house. Some belonged to Alexio and others to the owner of the house.

Alexio felt like he was going to be buried alive for ever. It took him less than five minutes to throw his few clothes into a suit-case. They drove back into the city. At the CID headquarters, the restriction order was read to Alexio. He was asked if he was in good health. He said yes he was. Freeman made him sign the restriction order.

By midday, Freeman, Bonga and another African detective called George, were on their way to Gwelo—a distance of about three hundred miles from Salisbury. Alexio was handcuffed the whole way to Gwelo. It was just after six o'clock in the evening when they arrived at Gwelo CID regional headquarters.

George, book him in,' said Freeman.

'Yes, Boss . . . Excuse me, Boss. Under what shall I book him?'

Freeman scratched his head for a few moments and said:

' "Immigration". Put him in the special room. Understand, George? If there is anyone there get them out to another cell.'

'Yes, Boss,' replied George.

Alexio was taken down into the basement of the building. He was told to empty out everything in his trouser pockets. He did. He was ordered to remove his jacket, shoes and socks. George unlocked the cell and shoved Alexio in. The heavy door clanged loudly behind him.

Is there anyone else in here? No, you stupid. You heard Freeman tell George that if there was anyone else they should be moved out to another cell. Not even a window! Thought prison cells had high barred small windows! This darkness! It makes you lose your sense of balance. Just can't walk straight. Does this mean my crime is so serious? What crime? Well, what crime? You are a very strange creature. You ought to be angry. You *know* very well you haven't committed any crime. Shit, what kind of person are you? They killed Sam for nothing—nothing. They killed him free of charge. Maybe Sam wasn't the only one. In fact Sam hasn't been the only one. They can just kill you. Maybe they will. That is not funny. But what's the point of putting me here? Maybe to frighten you. Maybe they want you to go mad! That would be terrible. No. Let's think about this situation. How can they really believe something you have absolutely nothing to do with! So you think you are being clever! The next thing you will be telling me is how unfair it all is. Do you think if you were a white boy—if you were everything you are but black, would you be here? Well, that's not a subject for discussion either. How can you separate what's happening to you from what's happening to everybody else? Wait. There must be something in here. Can't just be a black and bare cell. Best thing is to crawl—systematically. Maybe they are watching. In this darkness? They can't see a thing. Never know. Special gadgets. Let's sit down.

You are scared. Only five minutes! You are a real coward! That's true. Who? Nobody knows I am here. Oh, God. Need a cigarette. Look, keep cool. It's bad enough to be locked but why do they have to lock people in a dark room? Do you remember Dr Manette in Charles Dickens' 'Tale of two cities'? The Bastille. Did he have a light in his cell? Well, what does it matter anyway. He went mad, didn't he. How long—this whole thing depends on you. Keep your head. You are not the first one, you know. It wasn't specially built for you. When you get out of here you will be: Alexio Shonga PG (Prison Graduate). If you get out, that is. So be mature. Oh, no! That's why all the smell. Shit and urine. I wouldn't mind if it was mine, but someone else's! That's unfair. Food? How about if I need help? Let's say I suffer from epilepsy? You mean they don't care, even if I died? Someone has to pay for

alcohol. Well, look man, find the wall first. OK, here it is. Now, it feels like the door is this way—it must be this way. You hear of people being locked up in small, small rooms—shit, they just don't know how happy they are. *Sadza!* I told you it was somewhere. And beans! Let's be careful with the relish. Maybe should count the beans and ration yourself. Yes. One. Two . . . Three . . . Oh, this is crazy. Just take one lump with five beans. It will go down. Well, well, well. This tells us something. They haven't forgotten you, that's for sure. This food means they are not going to let you die. So, just forget death for a while. This is good! They want you alive. There has to be a reason. If you can think what that reason is and work out a solution you will be my best friend for ever! Break, but don't break! So take your chance. After all this, you don't need to act too much. But you know how to act anyway. But if you really break, you are the loser . . . If you think twenty-five good thoughts and count to seven million, you have two lumps of *sadza*—all right, just count to seven million.

It was late in the afternoon when they came to take him out of the black cell. He had his hands over his eyes. George had his hands on Alexio's arm. They walked over the fifty yards or so to the offices building.

'What day is it, Sir?'

'Monday.'

'What—I mean, which Monday?

'What do you mean which Monday?'

'How long have I been here?'

'Shut up! I am being good to you and now you think you can ask anything. You are not the first one, you know. Others have even died!

'Where are we going?' asked Alexio.

'I told you to shut up!' yelled George just before they came to Freeman's office. Freeman was seated on an easy-chair. By now Alexio could open his eyes for a few moments at a time. George guided him to a chair and assisted him to sit.

'OK, Sergeant. You can go out now.'

'Yes, Sir.' replied George subserviently and walked out of the room. When Alexio opened his eyes, he was staring at the soles of Freeman's shoes. He rubbed his eyes before looking again. Freeman blew some smoke of his cigarette towards Alexio. Alexio had to believe. Freeman had his legs on the desk. Strapped over his white shirt, Freeman wore a holster. In it was a revolver.

'You have grown very fat since I last saw you, Alexio . . . Are you ready to talk?' Freeman asked.

'Yes Sir.'

'Good! When are you off to Moscow?' asked Freeman taking his legs off the table.

'. . . Sir, if I knew, if I knew anything about going to Moscow, I would have told you a long time ago. I don't want—'

'So you are still not ready to talk, eh? You are very tough', said Freeman sarcastically.

'Sir,—'

'Shut up! . . . See this?' he asked pointing the revolver at Alexio, 'I can put a bullet through your brains and no one will ever know. Do you understand?'

Freeman wasn't joking or playing a game.

'Yes Sir,' replied Alexio.

'Listen my boy, I have every intention of making you talk!' said Freeman standing up.

'Alexio, this is the only chance you have. For at least two weeks—fourteen days. I won't be seeing you again until fourteen days from today. So it's up to you. If you want to talk, talk now . . . Do you want to just tell me when you are going to Moscow?'

'If I knew, I would tell you.'

'Well, you don't leave me much choice. I have to send you back to your room. Don't expect water or food. Should we find you dead, goodbye my friend.'

Alexio was taken back to the black cell.

You are a fool, Alexio. A big fool! Fourteen days . . . Fourteen days? Why did he say that? Why did he have to tell me? I mean people don't say things like that for no reason. No food? No water? 'Should we find you dead, goodbye my friend', I am not a bloody fool Mr FREEMAN! FREE MAN! My name is Alexio Shonga. No. My name is Chikomborero

Shonga. Even if I see you in heaven, I will kill you. I will. Then Jesus Christ will come and with the assistance of Rev Cope, he will transfer me to Hell! But you will be dead my friend, Mr Freeman! You will see!

Have you ever contemplated suicide? No, that's a foolish thought. No, it's not. Shut up! This is not the place to discuss philosophy. I just wish people could switch themselves 'on' and 'off' to wake up and to go to sleep. Right now, the best thing would be to switch myself 'off' for the next thirteen days.

Later, the same day, George came to fetch Alexio. He took him to Freeman's office again.

'Sit down Alexio,' said Freeman in a rather civil voice.

The now thin and pale figure sat on a chair.

'Do you know that I really like you?'

'Yes, Sir—I mean, I didn't know.'

'George! . . . Go and get some meat-pies, bananas and a soft drink.'

Freeman gave George some money. George took the money and went out of the office.

'Do you want to have a bath?'

'Well, Sir, it doesn't really matter.'

Alexio guessed where all this was heading to.

'Of course it matters. A man needs a bath now and again. Alexio . . . I want to help you to help yourself. Now you don't have anybody to pay your school fees. I am quite prepared to pay your school fees and to give you some pocket money—about fifty pounds a month. But of course I would expect you to keep in touch with me regularly. Especially when you have news that you think might be interesting to me. You will be very foolish not to consider this.'

'Sir, I don't know how long I have been here in Gwelo. I feel a little confused. Of course, I can just say I want to work with you just to get out of prison. But then when I go out, I may change my mind. I shall be back in trouble again.'

'You sure will be.'

'On the other hand, I can refuse now but will probably regret it afterwards . . . I don't know. If it was possible, I would like to be allowed to think about it. It's very difficult to make a decision while I am in prison.'

'Don't think you can fool me!'

'I am not fooling—I can't fool you, Sir.' Alexio, with an honest face, was gambling well.

'All right. I believe you. I will put in a request for your restriction order to be revoked. It will take about a week. But I have discretional authority to let you out immediately. I am going to arrange with a friend of mine to keep you at his house for three days, after which you must give me your decision. You are not to leave the yard of my friend's house. You are not to leave Gwelo without the permission of the police. Do you follow?

'Yes, Sir.'

'Now, you go out and wait for George outside. After you have taken your food and your bath, I want you to come back up here. Okay?'

'Thank you, Sir.'

Greedily, Alexio ate the food. Was he about to become an informer? Eating the food, he felt like he was eating his conscience. But he still trusted himself. The bath was to be one splash of cold water from a bucket. He declined it. Soon, he went up to Freeman's office again.

Alexio was taken seven miles out of Gwelo, to Fletcher High School. It was the other school for Africans that went up to sixth form. There, he was surprised to stay in the school sick-bay for three days. That was to be Alexio's home until he heard from Freeman. The sick-bay was to be 'out of bounds' to students and the black nurse who ran it. A guard was also to be posted outside the sick-bay.

George, an African guard, and Alexio drove to the school. Alexio was worried sick about this prostitution of his beliefs; but he knew what he was doing. After their arrival there, the guard took up his post outside. George wanted to say a few things to Alexio.

'Listen to me, kid brother. I am a policeman. It's a job. When you see me, all you see is a policeman. But I am a man too. Even when we take over, we shall still need policemen. I am not trying to justify that all we do is right . . . Most of the time, I can understand what crime a person has committed.

But in some cases, like your case, I fail to understand. You don't know how sorry I feel about all this happening. You don't know how angry I feel! If my son wants to go to Moscow, why shouldn't he? If he wants to go to London or to America, why shouldn't he? I will let him go . . . Now, believe me, please. If there is anything I can do, I want to help! I will help.'

Alexio didn't know whether to believe George or not. Yes, George could help. George could be used. What he had said made sense, but how could Alexio feel sure. It was possible George had been instructed to play the game. But there wasn't much time. Of course, Alexio wasn't going to be an informer. So he was in trouble anyway. Alexio quickly decided to take the risk. But he would not do much unless George took a serious risk—a real commitment.

'Yeah, I think you could help me.'

'I want to. Just say.'

'Do you have a car?'

'Yes. But I don't have a licence.'

The answer was promising.

'But you can drive?'

'Yeah,' George nodded.

'Could you drive me to Salisbury?'

George hesitated and then said:

'It's a long way. But since you need to get there, I will.' Something told Alexio that George was being genuine. But why? Alexio talked as though he had the upper hand.

'What time do you finish work tomorrow?'

'Nine-thirty.'

'Day after?'

'Nine-thirty the whole week.'

'Do you think you could tell me your address?'

George told Alexio a Senga Township address. It was in the African police compound at Senga.

'Do you think you will be going out any evening in the next five days?'

'No, I won't . . . But, you know, there isn't much time if you are thinking of getting away. But you can hide at my house. Nobody will look for you there.'

George left Alexio debating the risk he was thinking of taking. Could he trust George? He was a hope.

On the Friday evening, Alexio got into bed early. The next day, he was supposed to confirm to Freeman that he agreed to being an informer.

One thing he had not discussed with George was how to get out of the sick-bay. What was to be done with the guard? Maybe that's where the battle was to begin. If necessary and if he could, he would kill the guard. But how? The solution would provide itself when the problem arose. He left it at that but kept his eyes on the guard.

About an hour and a half after Alexio had got into bed, the guard tip-toed to the bed. Alexio was frightened and wanted to ask the guard why he was creeping to his bed. But the guard didn't look as though he was going to harm him. The boy closed his eyes. The guard looked at him for a second or two before he decided to get out of the sick-bay. He tip-toed out. Alexio opened his eyes again. It was unbelievable! The guard did not go back to sit in his usual place outside the door! After a few seconds, Alexio got out of bed. It was Friday! There was always at least one beer party in Senga.

Calmly, Alexio got dressed. Calmly, he walked into the toilet. He took a deep breath and climbed on to the toilet seat. He opened the small window. It was a struggle to get out. The window was too small even for a thin man like him. But it was not obstacles like this which were going to stop him. After some time, he dropped onto the ground, outside the sick-bay. Alexio was committed. It was too late to change his mind. He wanted to run but instead, he walked towards Senga. The moon was riding a clear sky. He could see where he was going. He followed a small path that ran through long savannah grass. It was a strange walk. He met an old man on the path. They did not greet each other but for no reason at all, the man said to Alexio:

'My son, when you travel, unless someone calls your name, don't look back. Never turn back, young man.'

'Thank you,' said Alexio very startled. He thought about what the man had said all the way into Senga and until he found George's house. At George's house, he knocked on the door.

'George, let's go,' said the boy as though a definite arrangement had been made before.

'Are you drunk?' George asked.

'DRUNK?'

'Well, come in for a while.'

'There is no time, remember?'

'Yeah, sure.'

George went into the house and put on a jacket. He spoke a few words to his wife before he came out of the house.

'Where is your baggage?' whispered George.

'I don't have any,' replied Alexio plainly.

In a way George was afraid of Alexio. They drove out of the police compound towards Gwelo. They got into Gwelo without speaking to each other. George was driving towards the CID offices. As he came to the building, the car slowed and turned left. There, it stopped. The petrol tank was filled. The oil was checked, the air pressure in the tyres was adjusted and the windscreen was cleaned. George paid, started the engine and drove onto the main road to Salisbury.

Five miles outside Gwelo, the car was flagged down by the police. There was a road block.

'Where are you going? Why are you in such a hurry?' a uniformed white policeman demanded.

'Licence?'

George fumbled with some papers from his pocket.

'Here it is, Sir' he said.

He was drenched in sweat. Suddenly he added:

'No! No! I am sorry, Sir. That's not my—'

'It's all right, Sergeant. You may proceed.'

There it was. Being a policeman had saved them. George kept on sighing. He cooled down a bit until they came about half-way to Salisbury. This time an African policeman waved them onto the kerb. There were about twenty other cars.

George got out of the car and walked to where the policemen were interrogating several drivers.

'What's going on?' George innocently and confidently asked an African policeman.

'George!'

'. . . God, Ramba!'

Ramba and George gripped hands. George and Ramba had trained at the same police school at the same time. They had a long and very friendly chat. They promised to visit each other soon. George was allowed to drive on.

'You don't have to tell me what you are going to do, but what will you do in Salisbury?' George asked.

'I want to get to Goromonzi as soon as possible.'

'But I can drive you there.'

'Look, it's dangerous for me to know any of your places. But if it's any help, I might as well drive you to Goromonzi.'

'Really?'

'Positive.'

When they got into Salisbury, it was four in the morning. Driving through the lit city, George suggested they both wore hats. It would be difficult to be recognized as blacks. There were two hats on the back-seat. They went through Salisbury with their hats on. At Goromonzi, Alexio had no words with which to thank George.

'I wish I did it everyday, brother', said George.

'One day—'

'One day, Alexio . . . Bye.'

'A million thanks!'

George turned the car round and headed for Salisbury.

At Goromonzi, Alexio walked to Paul and Sarah's house and knocked on their bedroom window. Paul took no time at all to get out of bed and let Alexio in. For the next two hours, the African boy narrated all that had happened to him since he last saw his friends.

'I want to get to Makosa as soon as possible,' he finished.

'But what will you do there?' asked Sarah.

'It's home. That's where I come from, you know. It's my home. Something will work out when I get there. But I must get there.'

They started for Makosa right away. At nine o'clock on Saturday morning, Alexio was dropped off on the outskirts of Makosa. Paul and Sarah hoped Alexio would keep in touch with them. He promised he would.

Yes. Now, Alexio had committed an offence. Now he was

really on the run. This time, there were only two people for him at Makosa. First Joy. He had to see her to tell her. He was in a mess. It was all over. What could he do? Next, of course, there was Chief Makosa. What would he say? Alexio did not know. There was certainly no point in seeing Gomo. No point at all.

Alexio managed to sneak into one of Joy's father's huts without being noticed.

'Thank the spirits of the ancestors! Thank the spirits of the ancestors! I went to Salisbury but couldn't find you? Where were you? What has been happening?'

Alexio told Joy the whole story.

'I have made up my mind about what I am going to do. It wasn't an easy decision to reach.'

'What are you going to do now?'

'I will tell you later. I don't think you will be very pleased.'

'You are going anyway.'

'Yes, Joy.'

'You are going to try and go to England.'

'I said I will tell you later.'

'Alexio? . . . Do you still love me?'

'Yes, of course. Why?'

'I have something to tell you.'

'Well, tell me.'

'I am—we are expecting a baby.'

Alexio was very pleased. They discussed what to do. He told her of his decision. It was pointless to get married. It would take a long time and there wasn't much time. Maybe they could marry later. But they decided to tell Joy's parents immediately. They knew that after explaining everything to Joy's father, he would understand why they couldn't marry. There was no choice.

Alexio's arrival at Makosa was a secret confined to Joy's family and Chief Makosa. If too many people knew about his presence it would lead to problems. After talking with Alexio and Joy, Joy's father went to Chief Makosa's huts. When he had finished eating the meal Joy had prepared for him, Alexio slept for a while. Later that afternoon, Chief Makosa came to see Alexio. Again, Alexio explained everything to Chief Makosa.

'Your mind is made up?'

'Yes, definitely.'

'When do you want to leave?'

'The longer I stay here, the more dangerous it is. The police must be looking for me.'

'Since you were last here, things have changed. Two, sometimes three times a week, soldiers and policemen raid the village. We have somebody who always tells us when they are coming. It's all right to stay here tonight but we must start at the first crow of the cock.'

Alexio and Joy had the rest of the day and the evening to themselves. They talked about everything but the future. They went to sleep very late.

Just after the first cock had crowed, Chief Makosa, carrying a ceremonial axe and a walking-stick, came for Alexio. It was still very dark when they left the village and headed for the hazy mountain range in the north. Chief Makosa knew the path very well.

'You will not be lonely up there. There are so many other young men. You will have very little time to worry. Now and again, I have to bring messages. I shall always bring you news of Joyce.'

It was a long walk. The Chief told Alexio what had been happening in the village.

'There is talk that the government is going to move us out of the village. But we shall fight before they can do that.'

Life in the mountains was not to be talked about to many outsiders. Alexio joined nearly four hundred other young men. They stayed there for seven months. After seven months, most of the young men in the mountains began to feel edgy. Everybody knew something was going to happen soon. Word had filtered through the bush into the mountains. The Party had issued the order. Excitement took over in the mountains. It was the end of a wait. A long wait.

A visitor soon arrived in the mountains. Chief Makosa had been arrested. Rumour had it that he had been killed by the police. There was much unrest at Makosa's village. Government soldiers were to set up a camp there the next day. They were to be taken before they entered the village.